TABLE OF CONTENTS

Although any returning DYSTOP-O-MART customers will [...] are no longer available, the World of Dystop-o-Mart isn'[...]

This 'season' we are proud to introduce our long-awaited D IS FOR DYSTOPIA ACTIVITY AND COLORING BOOK. Containing 86 pages of illustrations made by living Dystop-o-Mart employees and injured and honored product testers, this informative manual is used to color and contains activities to complete. This book is sure to be an irresistible distraction from the ongoing perils of your sad existence!

APOCAL-OOPS! A CHILDREN'S GUIDE TO MASS EXTINCTION

ILLUSTRATED GUIDE TO RADIATION SICKNESS
(A Paint-With-Water Book for Childish Adults)

DISCARDED APPLIANCES IN THEIR NATURAL ENVIRONMENT
(Coloring pages of our favorite scenic areas)

EVERYTHING IS DANGEROUS. (Nursery rhymes-n-riddles)

A DYSTOP-O-MART DAY PANNER
(A perpetual calendar that features "This Day in Misery," "Birthday/Sacrificeday," "DYSappointments," and "To Do or Don't List")

COMING SOON

Your style and survival demand it.
Whatever your direst need, Dystop-o-Mart
has something to sell you. SHOP NOW
SHOP NOW
SHOP NOW
SHOP NOW

TRANSPORTATION

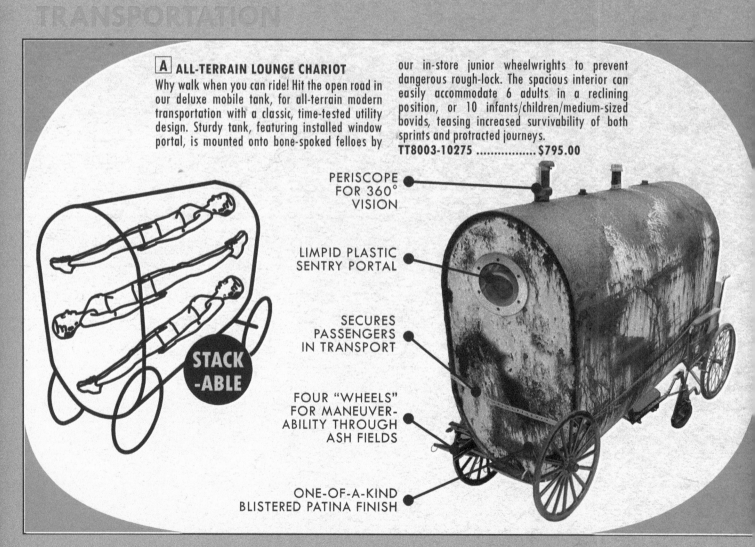

A ALL-TERRAIN LOUNGE CHARIOT
Why walk when you can ride! Hit the open road in our deluxe mobile tank, for all-terrain modern transportation with a classic, time-tested utility design. Sturdy tank, featuring installed window portal, is mounted onto bone-spoked felloes by our in-store junior wheelwrights to prevent dangerous rough-lock. The spacious interior can easily accommodate 6 adults in a reclining position, or 10 infants/children/medium-sized bovids, teasing increased survivability of both sprints and protracted journeys.

TT8003-10275 .... **$795.00**

PERISCOPE
FOR 360°
VISION

LIMPID PLASTIC
SENTRY PORTAL

SECURES
PASSENGERS
IN TRANSPORT

FOUR "WHEELS"
FOR MANEUVER-
ABILITY THROUGH
ASH FIELDS

ONE-OF-A-KIND
BLISTERED PATINA FINISH

STACK
-ABLE

PTP TRANSPORCHAIR
ALL-TERRAIN LOUNGE CHARIOT

TT546-23 PTP T-CHARIOT $3.95

Our PTP (Personal Transportation Pod) offers that special person in your life comfort and mobility, with unlimited MPG. Makes left and right turns. Fuel, add-ons, weather-resistant covering, and mud flaps may be available. Functional axles sold separately.

STORAGE FOR LIQUEFIED AND GASEOUS OXIGINATED COMPRESSION TANKS

VELVET-TOUCH SECURITY SNAP-AND-STRAP FIVE-POINT SAFETY HARNESSES

STEERING HANDLE AND MANUAL BREAKING SYSTEM

TEMPERATURESISTANT™ REUSABLE CUSHIONING

MASSAGING HEATED FOOTREST

ADJUSTABLE AXIS ALLOWS FOR RELAXING GYROTHEODOLIC RIDE

PERSONAL STORAGE BELLOW, IDEAL FOR STORAGE AND SMOKING OF FOODSTUFFS

A ZIP-KIT TRANS-PO-SYS

With the versatile Zip-Kit, you'll fly through the sky like a Super Nova! Safely traverse steaming lava pools, toxic fountains, and velociraptor habitats with speed, efficiency, and succor. Upcycled cable attaches securely to the edge of high-rising structures, bluffs, trees, wind turbines — any route you want to go! Connect point A to point B, and you've built a solution to your travel woes. Connect multiple instances of cables to the same location to create a transportation hub with various destinations; with Zip-Kit, the sky's no longer the limit!

The **Zip-Kit Base System** includes:
- Ten (10) meters of copper coaxial, multi-fiber launch, jumper cable, or litz wire, corrosively-eroded to a turbulence-free finish for minimal vibrationality during impactful descents.
- Hanger 4-pack Bundle supports single-rider weight of up to a whopping 50 Kilograms!
- Safety harness for suspending rider from the cable; extra crotch support means increased comfort and style

The **Z-Needs Executive Bundle** includes all of the features in the Base System, plus these exciting options:
- Three (3) jars of maderized French Dressing Line Lubricant: go faster than you ever dreamed or hoped was possible!
- Safety helmet (one size fits most): Incredible stopping power helps you stick the landing!
- Leak-resistant Reusable Absorption Garment: Allows reluctant riders to "rest" easy on their journey

ZIP-201 (Base System)..$895.00
ZIP-202 (Base System PLUS Z-Needs Bundle).......................$1,495.00
ZIP-203 (Extra 9-to-12 meters of cable).....................................$34.95
C ZIP-205 (One jar of French Dressing Line Lubricant) $6.95
B ZIP-207 (Reusable Absorption Garment) $11.95
ZIP-208 (Pre-printed Last Will and Testament Kit) $4.95

ABSORPTION GARMENT: GO ON THE GO!

FRENCH DRESSING LINE LUBRICANT FOR SPEED

SHELTER & DEFENSIVE LODGING

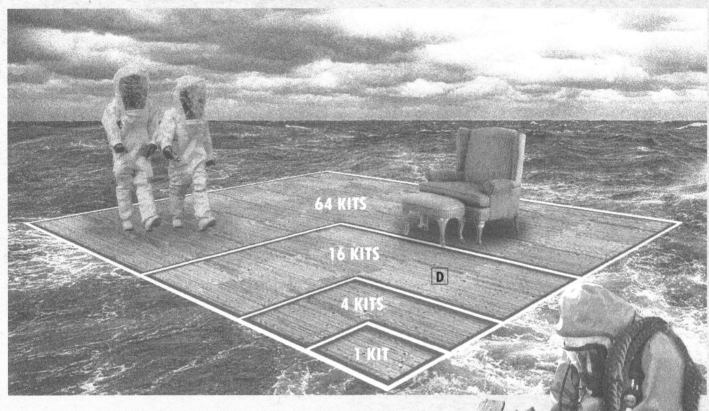

64 KITS

16 KITS

D

4 KITS

1 KIT

D YOUR OWN PRIVATE ISLAND

Cresting sea levels are forcing homeowners off of dry land and into luxurious oceanic privacy. With our build-your-own private island kit, you can enjoy the anodyne convenience of owning a slice of paradise! The extensible building kit is an interlocking system, so you can make your island as small or large as you like! Use the handy chart below to determine how many kits you'll need. Each kit contains: one (1) barrel containing radioactive gases to provide warmth; twelve (12) lengths of sturdy pallet wood for flooring; and 9 meters of rope, for modular assembly. Water-resistant. Some assembly required.

MODEL NUMBER	NUMBER OF KITS	SQUARE METERS	TOTAL PRICE
HOM-080	1	.55 m²	$62.00
HOM-081	4	2.23 m²	$239.00
HOM-082	16	9.00 m²	$949.00
HOM-083	64	36.00 m²	$3,795.00

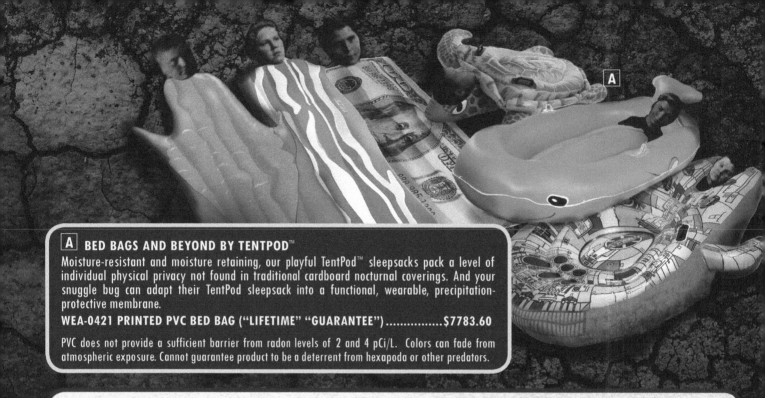

[A] BED BAGS AND BEYOND BY TENTPOD™

Moisture-resistant and moisture retaining, our playful TentPod™ sleepsacks pack a level of individual physical privacy not found in traditional cardboard nocturnal coverings. And your snuggle bug can adapt their TentPod sleepsack into a functional, wearable, precipitation-protective membrane.

WEA-0421 PRINTED PVC BED BAG ("LIFETIME" "GUARANTEE") $7783.60

PVC does not provide a sufficient barrier from radon levels of 2 and 4 pCi/L. Colors can fade from atmospheric exposure. Cannot guarantee product to be a deterrent from hexapoda or other predators.

[B] PRO-304 POPTENT™

Fabricated from heat, moisture, and gamma ray-resistant artisan industrial polyblend blankets, our best-selling PopTent offers you style — and a sense of security that's through the roof! Corinthian leather trim and patches help maintain meteorological comfort at a fraction of the cost of adaptive architectural reconstruction! Pair with TentPod™ sleep sacks for next-level comfort in protective sleeping pods, domes, caves, and burrows. 200 x 244cm; 2kg when dry.

PRO-304 .... $8.95

PopTent offers up to 2 adults and one child (or other) the kind of safety playa marauders only dream of.

"FOR CENTURIES, TENTS WERE THE GO-TO CHOICE FOR SMART HOUSING. WITH SECUR-I-RING™, WE NOW REST LESS AFRAID!"
—Miendsta Jacksonner, mother

[C] GLASS SECUR-I-RING / TODDLER 'CHARD'N OF DELITES™

Finally a security system for the whole family! An anti-personnel playstation to protect toddlers or other valuable resources. 100% recycled "recycled" glass, sourced from our exclusive private restitution centers, showcases light-sensitive multicolored shards affixed to industrial-strength — but surprisingly lightweight — steel corrugated cable wire spool flanges — that fold up for needed transport.

HOM-15 .... $429.95

[D] TODDER SUSPENSION CARRIAGE (Seasonal Avail.)
HOM-18 .... $99.95

Cross-section of PopTent with Glass Secur-I-ring protection system

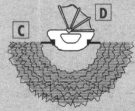

Toddler Suspension Carriage mounted to Glass Secur-I-ring protection system. Style may vary based upon availability.

E SCALY PLASTIPEDIC

Upcycled bedding-mix available in twin, full/queen, Junta Jr™ or Junta+ sizes. Contact-free self-delivery requires flatbed vehicle or other conveyance.

CC72-5 ....$99.95

F CONVERT-A-BUILD E-Z POP-UP PARKING VILLAGE PODS

With the new Convert-a-Build housing system, overnight parking is a "lot" easier! Our convenient shelter pod provides an ideal overflow solution: as the need grows for more space, just add pods for the perfect weekend escape. Leak-resistant enclosure construction may shield against acid rain, rabid beasts of prey, thieves, miscreants, yak-killers, and murder hornet attacks. *Parked pods may be scattered randomly in a no in-lieu-free, rustic camocamp approach (or angled, perpendicular, parallel, single- or double-row) to avoid blind spots.*

HOM-790 (base pod).................................$1,495.00
HOM-792 (two-tone glass) $89.95
HOM-795 (moonroof)......................................varies
HOM-795 (Insta-Drain™, 1 square yard).........$49.95

Each pod features:

- Our patented Predator-Vision™ Wind "Shield" — transparent for easy viewing, allowing you to keep an eye out for human and animal intruders, while maintaining a physical safety barrier
- Distinctive distressed craquelure effect supports identifiable details for contested ownership
- Pre-formed Air-Port™ holes promise aeration for easier respiration
- Seasonal two-tone glass *(not available in many habitable zones)*
- Predatory-alert moonroof available at extra charge *(contact manufacturer directly for availability)*
- Our Insta-Drain!™ Effluvient Runoff Ground Tarp may keep you high and dry *(sold separately)*

INSTA-DRAIN™
EFFLUVIENT RUNOFF TARP

AIR-PORT™ HOLES
FOR AERATION

INTEGRATED MIRRORS FOR
EXTRA SURVEILLANCE

FAMILY CADAVER DISPOSAL

Canatorium

A YOU "CAN" AFFORD A MAUSOLEUM

Maybe it's a total stranger. Maybe it's a family member — who can be sure? Either way you've got human remains to take care of. It's time for Canatorium! The E-Z solution to remains any day! Just dry the remains, pack the Canatorium, and kindle. The unique properties of the unit will keep you and remaining family members alive for temperatures down to 15°C! Then just wait for the "Can" to cool, label, and you "can" easily assemble a durable windbreaker maus"oil"leum!

FCD-020 CANATORIUM MORTUARY CAN $239.95
FCD-021 CANATORIUM MORTUARY CAN (1 DOZEN) $2504.60
FCD-022 CANATORIUM SEALING KEY $639.95
FCD-023 RUBBER GASKET (moisture and pest deterrent)...................... $47.99
FCD-024 LAVENDER + PAEDERIA FOETIDA ASH SCENT
(28.35g container, not included)... $17.85

B PORTAMORGUE

They say it's all death and taxes! And now, with smaller shadow government, you can afford to honor your dead! Whether those beloved remains are a pet or a limb, this mortuary-on-the-go will always be there. *(Not vermin proof.)*

PTM-001 MORTUARY CAN $217.99

C BAÑO BOMBAS

With our new and improved bath bombs, a badly-needed "spa day" is a blast! Sustainably-harvested pinecones are infused with nitrocellulosic compounds in our exclusive process, then kissed with just an extra pinch of banana scent for an aromatherapeutic delight. Build your spa in three easy steps:

1. Light your Baño Bomba fuse using any available fire-making technology

2. Throw your Baño Bomba into a clearing, preferably unpopulated, with a minimum of radioactive structures; explosive power will create the perfect-size hole for your new spa!

3. Wait for the resulting blast hole to fill with precipitation, then sit, soak, and enjoy!

Not recommended for children under 6 weeks.

N9924-86729G............................... $29.95

LIGHT

BOOM

SOAK

CAMP CARE

D HIDE-AWAY ANIMAL TOWELS

Step out of your bayou and into indulgent comfort with our fluffily absorbent-like former animal towels. We source our hides from the youngest supply available, for scar-free appearance and low-abrasion texture. Freshly-skinned and par-boiled, these reusable towels can, in a pinch, also be a long-lasting jerky treat. *Odiferous cadaverine emanations and oleaginous discharge will lessen with persistent usage.*

HNH-31 Seal Pup, Bath Towel..............................$69.95
HNH-34 Platypus Puggle (or similar), Hand Towel $49.95
HNH-33 Sup-r-Soft Rabbit Kitten, Washcloth $34.95

E ON-AND-OFFAL REMOVAL MATS

Humorously abrasive! Spruce up your *portes de la mort;* hedgehog thorns are woven onto Baltimore ballast, then lacquered with kupilu nutmeal to slap-on a scant soupçon of shanty status.

HNH-0120 LIVE, LAUGH, LOVE $19.95
HNH-0124 PLEASE SCRAPE NUBS BEFORE ENTERING $19.95
HNH-0131 CAUTION: LOOSE STOOL $19.95

F "WELCOME"/"DO NOT ENTER" SHIELD

Safety shield alerts guests to inevitable danger. Encircled with spent ammunition for a jocund appearance. Pressed pigmented tin cloisonnéd with wombat secretions.

HNH-1329...$49.95

G TOASTEE™ CIRCLE

Heat your home the faith-based way, with the comforting glow and lasting warmth of flames! Our Toastee™ Circles scorch even during deluges to smoke out those nuclearic winter chills. Integrated plastic cooking spikes surround the perimeter and double as a cradle. Burns for 1 to $1\frac{1}{32}$ hours.

TST-2771 (single circle)....................................$5.95
TST-2772 (4-pak) $26.95

H PEEPOT®

We all know radiation is diarrhetic. But traditional bedside urine containers and bedpans don't guard you and your family from the risks of urinactive exposure. Some families even risk leaving their shelter to relieve themselves, but we all know that risk is too great! With PeePot®, your whole unit can rest better knowing that 30-35% of urine radionuclides are safely contained. *(Not tested on hydrogen-3 [tritium], carbon-14 and strontium-90.)*

HNH-40086...$79.95

From our tent, to yours!

CAMP CARE: THE GREAT OUTDOORS

A **PRO-TKT REVERSIBLE SOLAR RADIATION SHIELD AND E-Z-BAQUE SUNSHINE OVEN**

Protect yourself from plummeting sky-borne perils! Our easy-to-deploy shield is lined with Reflect-O discs for optimized defense against: Electromagnetic Radiation (including X-Rays and Ultraviolet bombardment); Brainwave Radio-control Emissions; Errant 8G signals; jorogulls; and Chemtrail Dustings. But wait, there's more! Rotate 180° and the shield transforms into our proprietary solar oven! *Sold separately. See page 15 for details.*

PF-0050.............................$69.95

B **SIMMERSOAKER HOT POT**

Preparing a meal has never been more relaxing! Call a time-out from guarding the offspring and sink into flavor. Sauté those detached muscles and prepare rations at the same time! Inextinguishable metal construction transmits geothermal heat to both your body and your meal.

PF-0017.............................$225.00

You'll "lava" our bargains!

C BARNAKL BASKIT YONI STEAMER

Rare, wire mesh rideshare bin thaws barnacles, carapaces, and fishy biomass. *Crush hazard.*

PF-8227...............................$899.95

D CONVERSATION PIT SEATING

Don't be stumped when it comes to heated seats! Enjoy this comfy auto oasis with other gridlocked guests. Vintage cold-pressed "auto-stabiles" absorb the toughest environmental elements, and offer a toasty, compact surface for seating, dining, and parrying predators.

PF-8962...............................$99.95

E THUNDER MUG

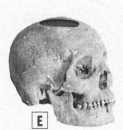

Employ this galvanic piece of bone china barware for gulping fluids—whilst smiting one's enemies. *Cranial chalice may vary due to genetics, developmental delays, and environmental effluence.*

PF-2551...............$14.95

F "MISS L." CASING INSULATED SAMOVAR

Stop pouring liquid into your pockets! Undetonated™ ammocarafe holds your drink in one place. Our metal flask keeps your liquid hot or cold for over ½ hour. Also makes a surprisingly incendiary dowry device!

PF-2558...............................$12.95

G MYLAR ALFRESCO BLANQUETTE

Made of repurposed reconaissance bladders, this protective picnic tarpaulin discourages fire ant hordes and terapedes. Shiny!

PF-0017...............................$9.95

H TOI-TOSS TOY – MULTI-MODALITY STRENGTHENING GAME

Pre-seasöned antique lavatorial seating unit is hurled at durable uchannel pöst (not included) for mönths of musubi-dachi merriment.

PF-0103...............................$6.95
PF-0118 POTTY-PITCH TEETHERS..........$15.95

I SON SCREEN™

Don't let deceased children go to waste. Our patented, portable youth incineration system provides a rich supply of slag for personal atmospheric protection. Ask your Dystōp-o-Mart representative about how you can use Son Screen™ for building and sporting projects!

HNH-SPV3.....................$119.95
HNH-SPV5 NOSEPLUGS
(Not pictured) $29.95

J INCONSOLABLE HUMAN/BIRD–HYBRID STATUARY MONUMENT

HNH-90 ....$499.95

IT'S BED™ TIME

K THE FLOWER BED™

The perfect foam-action moisture-harvesting germination incubator! Just add ticks to your crop of lice eggs, and dinner is on its way! Not only a hotbed of nutrition, The Flower Bed is *also* an irresistible predator attractor and catch-all. The rusticated spring-action coils retain and trap invading possums, rats, scorpions, slugs, and other delicacies and possibly other foodstuffs. With unlimited food acquisition potentiality, everyone just might catch some zzz's after their flower bed feast! *(Condition may vary.)*

GAH-002 FLOWER BED $2,213.99

WONDERFUL WORLD OF COLORS

  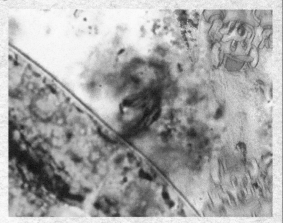

Sometimes we forget to look around. All the marvelous colors! Have you ever stopped foraging to just really look at rotting algae? It's like a methane rainbow! Well why not bring some color, or even your childhood memories, "home"?! Our limited edition multi-media "prints" may not only protect you and those with you from deadly solar flares, but add a little color into your holiday cohabicontainer divider! *Fabricated using our own exclusive quartzited salt boards. Ranging from 500 mm to 1 landing field etchings (rubber on encrusted quartzited salt).*

HNH-448 Assorted images (subject matter may vary)........ Price Seasonal

PULLEYPALOOZA!

"THEY WOULD BE EATEN IN THAT SINKHOLE IF IT WEREN'T FOR YOUR REEFURBISHED PULLEYS"
— T. S. 43900D, paternal guardian

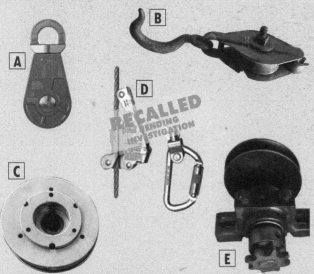

Who's gettin' hungry?! Whether you need to hoist a carcass for skinning or perform surgical procedures, you know that our pulleys are roof-raisers.

A | CSDRNFPA SECURITY PULLEY™
Static-pro for general 12.5mm use with screw-lock carabiners, (locking mechanism not included).
2℧R-PU202 .... $8.95

B | STEELWHEEL "BLOCK 'N' TACKLE" METAL-LIKE PULLEY WITH WORKING HOOK
Every household needs one. Can suspend up to a party of five. Adjustable tension "bolt".
2℧R-PU203 .... $2,999.95

C | 96-00 UNDERDRIVE "STALLION"
In a pinch can be used as a wheel or weaponry discus.
2℧R-PU204 .... $285.95

D | SAD LAF SLEEVE
Pocket-size perfection for emergency rescue or latchkey infant.
2℧R-PU204 .... $502.15

E | PULLY AND SPROCKET ASSY
Averts ventilation door cable breakage which can save lives during solar flare-related electrical blizzards.
2℧R-PU205 .... $1488.99

OFFENSE

"BEE-ZOOKA" BEE BEE GUN

You'll be one honey of a shot with the weapon beepeacekeepers and perimeter guards are buzzing about! Load up with organically-harvested munitions—honeybees, murder hornets, stinging wasps—and your enemies will feel your buzz-tastic sting! In under sixty pumps, compressed air propels ammunition with explosive force in the general direction of the target, and the wide dispersal pattern guarantees that even 18-month-old Acacius can effectively take out their target. Actuating honey port dispenses viscous nectar into the palm of your glove or isolator, for extra bee-serking accuracy! It's a sweet deal all-around!

H DEF-501 "BEE-ZOOKA" BEE BEE GUN.......................................$269.95

I DEF-502 HONEYBEES (Not pictured)
Sold in 1kg slubbed linen sacks for portability.....................$119.95

J DEF-504 MURDER HORNETS Readily available at no additional
charge inside the Dystōp-o-Mart employee lava cone.................FREE

K DEF-507 WEAPONIZED HUMMINGBIRDS (Not pictured)
Didja know these toxic little missiles become deadly when ravenously hungry? Pick up a couple of these pocket-sized projectiles!
Handling without protective helmet is guaranteed fatal. $59.95

L DEF-618 SAFETY HELMET Convincingly suggests protection
against larger insects and pouncing mutagenic waterfowl $2,172.95

M PLUTONI-YUMS

Radiation isn't going anywhere soon! Make the mighty atom work for you by ridding yourself of any annoyance in a tasty, speedy way! Why compete for provisions, for dating, for bedding? Thin the herd, the lemon-flavored way.

Artifical flavor. Indiv. candies should be handled only by intended consumer. HEMATOPOIETIC SYNDROME ensured; Nugget contains 0.8 Gy — that's more than 70 savory rads! Body disposal should meet Prop Crisis 65 exposure standards.

WEA-021 LEAD-WRAPPED LOZENGE (1EA).......................................683.60

N AERIAL DEFENSE NUNCHUCK

Combined initial velocities between the attacking prey and the nunchuck use linear momentum with destructive force, quickly and safely eliminating airborne threats to your kin and camp. Weighted handle offers secure gripping point and heavy-duty interlocking chain link kusari accentuates centripetal forces for stunning results. Plastic exterior is dishwasher safe, allowing easy removal of blood, cartilage, and sinew.

DEF-960............................$89.95

STOPS BIRD AT-TACKS

DEFENSE

D COOK-N-SHOOT POTATO CANNON

Home defense has never been so palatable! Our potato cannon is constructed of recovered PVC piping, and mounted onto vintage farm МОТОбЛОК for easy maneuvering. Plutonium-238-powered radioisotope thermoelectric generator provides the energy and heat you need to boil, fry, and even bake the potatoes, before launching them as defense projectiles. *Mashed potatoes not recommended for defense.*

CANNON
PRO-040 ....$9.95

POTATO CROQUETTES (24) (Not pictured)
PRO-041 .... $183.60

WARM POTATO SALAD SEASONING PACK
(Not pictured)
PRO-042 ....market price

E FRENCH FRY TUBERDAPTER

Shown above. Makes fries in our signature hexagonal shape! Oxidized poultry netting, held in 100% synthetic polyvinyl frame, for easy attachment and removal.

PRO-043 ....$18.95

F PRO-TKT REVERSIBLE BUMBER-BRUT
SUNSHINE OVEN AND SOLAR RADIATION SHIELD

Harness the power of exospheric degradative cycles, and bake prey while the sun shines! Our easy-to-carry portable oven is lined with Reflect-O discs for optimized focusing of full-spectrum cooking energies. Place edible substance on the convenient Stabilo-Spike prong, aim towards the sunshine, and in 5-7 days you'll have a perfectly-roasted feast! The Sunshine Oven captures Electromagnetic Radiation for even cooking, down to the bone, and X-Rays and Ultraviolet emissions roast and tenderize the foodstuff to an acceptable level of browning and crispiness. But wait, there's more! Rotate 180° and the solar oven transforms into a shield! See page 10 for details. *Fowl not included.*

PF-0050............................$69.95

G MARITIME CONTROL DEFENDER

Rising tides mean more tetrapods from the deep——and that's good eatin'! Defend and feed your camp with one easy swing. Weighted head adds increased angular velocity to crack the chitinous carapace of sea scorpions, marina spiders——even vampire crabs! —— without fouling the precious flesh.

PRO03-90 ....$39.95

Serving Suggestion

PERMA-BOOTZ by HOOFERS Holding Limited

"NEVER GO SHOE-LESS AGAIN"

- Perma-Bootz filled with enveloping security powder; just add moisture to activate tumescent concrete!
- Theft-proof lifetime-warranty-engineered cementitious composite
- Footwear linings sold separately.
- When used on livestock or personal support staff-members, Perma-Bootz have been reported to be 70% effective in averting hegira or other attempted exit strategies.

CL-PB26 (Left foot)........................ $189.95

B **YELL-OW CAKE LIMBWARMERS**

YELL-OW 污泥饼 CAKE

Hypothermia is murder on your skin; stay toasty in even the most inhospitable magnetic-evaporative cold front. Look absolutely stunning at absolute zero!

Our own locally-leached uranium ore hugs your limb in a dispensable distensible, flattering fluid-resistant netted cozy. Slow-release spallation effectively distracts from aches, while exfoliating unsightly eschars. Give frostbite the third-degree! *Not intended for reheating leftovers.*

CL26-5.................................. $89.95

CLOTHING

CHUNKY

HEAT 'N' EAT WEARABLE SINGLE-USE ELECTROSTATIC DISCHARGE ATTRACTOR

This single-use particle beam collector captures enough energy to heat four-to-six handfuls of liquid to over 20°! Your cares, worries, and limbs will melt away as you're accelerated into a sapid repast for your entire camp. You'll be a locavore hero — braised and praised between each toothsome bite. Guaranteed neat eatin': better than bat and stork shoulder! Lather up beforehand with our optional saucy lotions for a flavor boost and astringent skin peel. And, butter makes it better: our enema butt-r bag adds a complexity that secretes through every mouth-watering pore.

C **FOIL SUIT AND ÉPÉE COMBO**
Exterior wrap retains moisture and fluids
SDC51-003 .... $499.95

D **AKRON-STYLE BARBEQUE LOTION**
Say "yee-haw" to redolent flavor. *May be habit forming.*
SDC51-005 .... $19.95

E **NEWARK LIMONATA LOTION**
The taste of the tropics; sun-kissed citrus-y bouquet
SDC51-006 .... $19.95

F **CHICKEN KIEV BUTT-R FLAVOR ENEMA BAG**
Insert prior to exposure; electrical discharge lubricates internal comestibles into an indulgent slurry.
SDC51-008 .... $39.95

CLOTHING

A WAVELENGTH JAMMING HEAD UNIT

Keep stray 7G rays and bioweaponized influencers out of your compromised braincase. Former data repositories meet modern quantum tech to reflect and diffuse nocturnal bandwith emissions, preventing biological synaptic plasticity with legacy microchip implants. Spectral diodes combat ineluctable smishing wavelengths with aeromedical countermeasures. Sickly-styled with shielding wiry mesh and covertient electrical-absorption nodules. Powered by 132 AA batteries (not included or manufactured).

SDC86-003..............$89.95

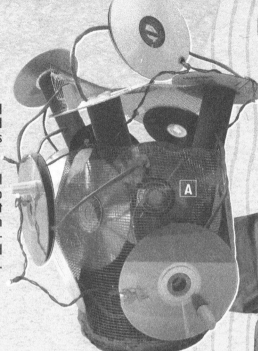

B FECAL DRIFT CONCERT GARMENT

Your relatives have endured hardship and starvation, but you had to embark on your three-season pilgrimage to the concert venue in Tropical Winnipeque. You've saved up four mammal offerings and risked procuring a ticket from a scalper. Now, your relatives demand proof of your attendance. Your purchase of this actinic keratoses-resistant garment also helps fund the Barrelsville Edwinston Family Foundation.

SP820-04 (1 ea) $149.95
SP820-05 (half-size) $74.975

> **"I wouldn't dare make the mistake of stepping outside without Dystōp-o-Mart life-elastic fashions!!"**
>
> —Mary Bernerd
> Ansthojour., DDTS

C BURIAL JAMMIES™

Artistically-grown mixed-phyla fungus outerwear. E-z care: self-repairing bullet-and-shrapnel hole "fabric" — just add liquid! Protective layer is fungus gnat resistant. *Avoid tactile contact with outer layer. May not be edible. Not vermin proof.*

SP218-01....................$279.95

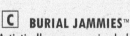

NOT AVAILABLE

NOT AVAILABLE

SOLD SEPARATELY

INTIMATES

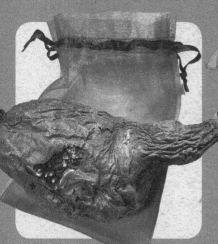

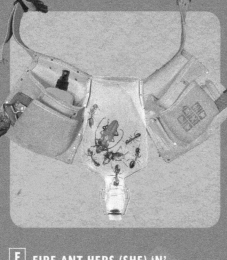

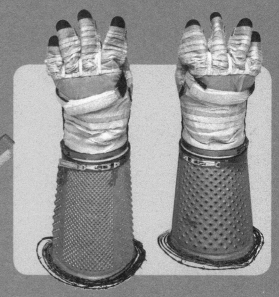

E MENSTRO MEAL™

Dystōp-o-Mart's Menstro Meal is wildly popular, thanks to the daintily-liberating estrogenic properties of periodically-obtained traditional Oregonian eel meal.

CM5-61 Dowry pouch sack $24.95
CM5-62 40g tub $584.95

F FIRE ANT HERS (SHE) 'N' HIS (HIM) CHASTITY BELTS

Fighting fire with fire! Your suitor is unlikely to succumb to libidinous fever if you gird your loins with this reusable fits-most-sizes unibelt. The imported insectae in this easily-broken terrarium promise to assuage unwelcome advances. Handy pockets can provide storage for other tools and bribes. Break glass to easily activate defensive measures. *Do not rinse eyes. Abstinence is not guaranteed.*

CM5-82.......................................$55.00

D LADY DAY DISH SCOURS

Thermal pools are synonymous with containerwashing, but can eat right through your hand's integumentary system. This pulchritudinous accessory is a contempo marriage of form, function, surety, comfort, and éclat. Stained steel grates tackle tough food chars. And, a barbed cuffcoil keeps biting insects from nesting in the scour hand-socket. Because, cleanliness *is* survivalness!

CM5-15 1 left (ea)...................................$74.95
CM5-16 1 right (ea)..................................$74.95
CM5-17 1 nub (ea)....................................$14.95
CM5-18 1 child/other (ea)..........................$1.95
CM5-19 1 plasticine scrubflower (ea)........$84.95

G 2-IN-1 GENITAL SUSPENSOR & FACE MASK

Why choose when you can have both! Thick, absorbent Corinthians 2:6 leather wicks away moisture and odors, protecting genitalia by providing projectile dysfunction. Then, rotate it 180° and use as a face mask when traversing toxified swamps. Avoid inhaling mephitic gases through mouth and nose! Decorative white sticky-stripes trap annoying and/or deadly insects. Constructed of 100% pre-owned materials.

CM03-08 Main unit $29.95
CM03-15 Sticky-Stripe
          Reactive Gum (1 jar)......... $2.95

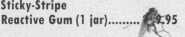

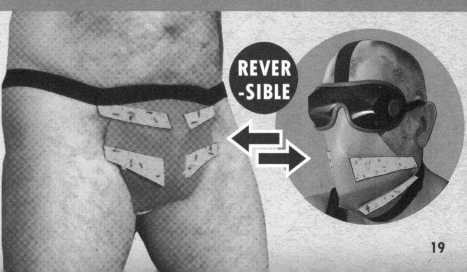

REVER-SIBLE

Handy Household Must-Haves

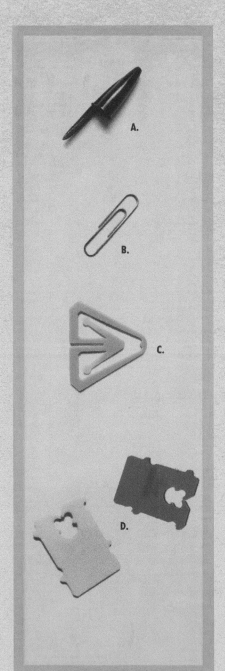

A.

B.

C.

D.

A LICE AND GINGIVAL INSTRUMENT
Also useful for scraping of annoying squamous scabs!
HH03-63 ....$17.95

B POCKET ALL-IN-ONE TOOL "CLIPPY"
is ready to help. From toxic undernail residue to resetting land mines, finger or toe splint. *CAUTION: Given the unreliability of shifting gravitational poles, we advise against employing this tool to manufacture a makeshift, floating-leaf compass.*
HH03-64 ....$3.95

C FASHION ACCESSORY
Less useful for scraping of annoying squamous scabs.
HH03-65 ....$17.95

D CLASPS
Millions of uses. Assorted colors.
HH03-66 ....$4.95

E ANTIQUE WHATCHAMACALLIT
Whether you call this classic a 47', CP47', bullet, ammo, or "clothespin", this vintage tool is a keeper. Made of real wood. As available.
HH03-67..........................$34.95

F RUBBER LOOP
Authentic. Perfect for tourniquets and toddler locks; might be melted to use as a suture.
HH03-68..........................$6.49

G POLLINATOR
Has anyone in your camp ever seen wild-flowers? You'll "bee" the toast of your towne when you whip out your "tipsy stick" to pollinate 'em! More flowers means more insects — and more insects may mean more food!
HH03-69..........................$8.49

H TWISTER
Everyone has something that needs to be bound. Not waterproof.
HH03-70..........................$8.79

USEFUL

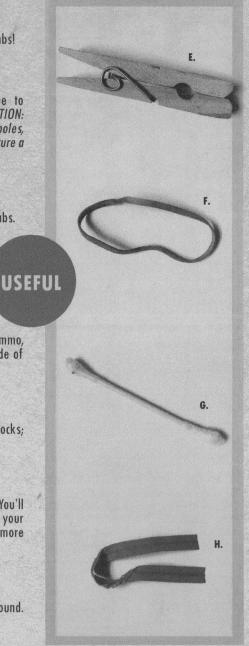

E.

F.

G.

H.

Personal Fandangles

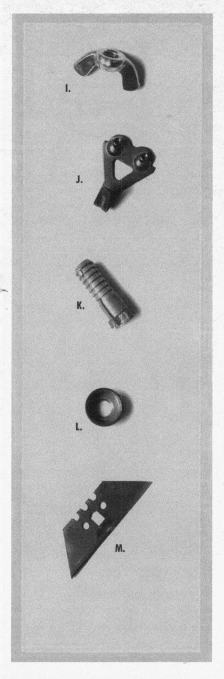

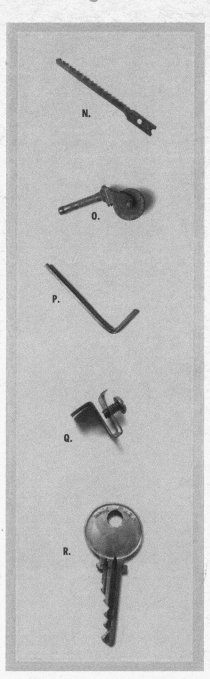

I METAL-PLATED WING-NUT
May not fit some percings or threaded screws.
HH03-71..........................$188.99

J ID HOLDER
Perfect for those who want everyone to know their status. (Neck string sold separately.)
HH03-71..........................$8.49

K POCKET SALIVA/VENOM SUCTION TUBE
May help eliminate the daily itching, stinging, and swelling that occurs with insect bites & mortar rounds.
HH03-73..........................$68.49

L MINI-SIREN
Help ward off deadly insects and fowl with this hand-held whistle. *Pitch may attract corybantic carnivores.*
HH03-74 38-44 kHz Model..........................$4.89

M POWER GRABBER
Celebrate your territorial dominance with this powerful reminder of your battle prowess. Protective scabbard not included.
HH03-75..........................$367.09

N FINE ZIG-ZAG PENDANT
Not tested as effective for endemic warfare purposes.
HH03-76..........................$14.49

O POCKET SPINNER
Toddler toy and teether.
HH03-77..........................$14.49

P TRADITIONAL IKEAN FINGER SPLINT
Attractive "L" splint. Can also be adhered to most ceremonial garments. Not for piercing or surgical use.
HH03-78..........................$14.49

Q PINCH PIN
Adjustable screw-tightened replacement snap.
HH03-79..........................$14.49

R GOOD-LUCK LOCKET ORNAMENT
Symbolic, heirloom zig-zag saw-tooth pendant.
HH03-80..........................$1694.49

DYSTŌP-O-MART SURVIVORIUM

PICK-UR-OWN
TERRA-GATED "FUN ZONE"

Are you the envy of your camp?
Visit the "fun zone"! Includes:

- **petting zoo hospice**
- **louseatorium**
- **vivisection Buffet**
- **custodial rep lounge area**
- **toilet facilites**

See page 24 for contraindications.

CHOLERA COVE WATER PARK

Explore the chemistry of the deep in our watertable of biotic mystery. Quiver in feverish excitement! Kicking the bucket list has never been more refreshing. Discover artifacts from bygone ages. Diving gear not allowed.

VISIT THE COMPOUND FOR EPOCHS OF FUN!

VAGI-VET BURDETTE'S KOZY-KASKETS

From graveyard to "Stay yard!" Repose in comfort and safety in repurposed caskets. Earthen berms absorb gamma radiation while you slumber, and geothermal heating exudes warmth into weary bones. It may not be your final resting place, but you'll wish it were! Decor and amenities vary per zone.

FREE PARKING !!

BURSTON BELLIE'S UNDERGROUND HIDEAWAY FARM -N- HOMESTEAD
Prime Agrarian Properties For Rent And Lease

Do pesky marauders "help themselves" to your live-stock? Not with your new underground farm-n-homestead!! Keep your pets and produce out of harm's way. Your animals remain safe. *Many animals* love *tunneling; exercise extreme caution in mine-field wing.*

- **Bioturbation crop-swap leases available**
- **Factory Farm Safe Space scum-well sewers (with our nutrient and mineral-rich runny water) for animal maintenance.**

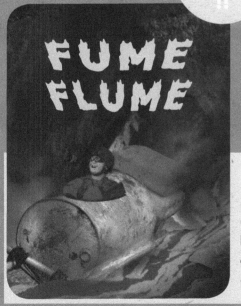

FUME FLUME

THE FUME FLUME™ LAVA TUBE RIDE

Dystōp-O-Mart's hottest attraction; now admitting adventurous explorers! Cruise down the lava tube in our specially-equipped heat-resistant containers, and enjoy scenery as sizzling miasma clears skin pores and unlaxes tired muscles. Guaranteed to be educational, entertaining, and exfoliating!

HOW TO ORDER
. . . THE DYSTŌP-O-MART WAY!

BY COURIER
Affix meat offering to order form, then input trans-cranial subduction hypnosis to record the following parcel address into nearest courier turtlebot's term memory:

Dystōp-O-Mart
Attn: Order Compartment
Cheyenne Mountain Shopping Annex
Prefecture-Level City, HZ1
NA Quarantowne Quadrant

BY SMOKE SIGNAL
On a typhoon-free day, send the following message via smoke signal:

.... .. / .. / -. . . .-. --.. / ... .-- -- .
/ ... - ..- ..-. ...- ..-. / .. .- -.. / - .... .. -. ... --. .
/ ..-. .- --- -- / -.-- --- ..-.. / -... .- --.-
/ ... --- / ..-. -. -. ./ ..-. --- ... / --- .- .--- ... -... .
/ .---- ..- ... . / ..-. / - .- / -- .. -. . ... .
/ .--. .-.. --.. / .- -. - .. -. ... / .- .-.
/ - .... --. ... / -- / .- - ..- -.. / ... .-. -..

There is a high probability that a fourth-party may intercept this message. To include payment, affix meat and trinkets to a mollusk wing for reported increased delivery success probability.

VISIT OUR SHOWHUT
Visit us and experience the splendor* of the Dystōp-o-Mart product range. No entry allowed without protective footwear or unaccompanied children.

OUR GUARANTEE
A Dystōp-o-Mart guarantee is aimed to protect our customers in all ways. Merchandise is guaranteed to be somewhat similar as represented in this catalog, with the exception of satisfaction. We proudly guarantee that the quality of all our products is optional.

OUR SHOPPING GUARANTEE
When Dystōp-o-Mart had pioneered shopping in Habitable Zone 1 and surrounding areas, it guaranteed that you would continue to procure any article illustrated in this catalog, as long as that item is in stock AND our warehouse shipping complex is fully operational AND Dystōp-o-Mart is still an operating concern AND Dystōp-o-Mart founders comply with aforementioned terms and/or conditions and/or constraints and/or meteorological variances.

We wish to call your attention that there have been many price increases in foodstuffs/metals/woods/arachnids in recent months.

We always endeavor to sustain prices illustrated in this catalog when possible and assuming present stock is available — and then, and only then — will replacement merchandise be supplanted with pricing reflective of economic equilibrium.

This catalog has been several hours in preparation. Therefore, it is certain that many prices will already have increased, as well as many products discontinued and/or missing from inventory. Disputes waivered upon your submission of receipt of this catalog's warranty.

ENEMIES RUN IN FEAR FROM SAVINGS

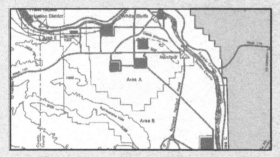

UP-TO-DATE HAZARD MAPS AVAILABLE

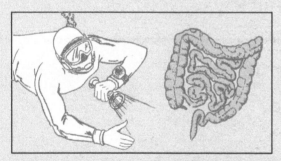

DIVE INTO THE SMALL AND LARGE GRAB BAG

- BENZODIAZEPINES
- BIOTIN
- GUD EATZ CAFF-FINE™
- DEXAMETHASOLIDS
- EUKODAL
- FOLATE
- NICOTINE
- REGENEUROIDS
- GUD EATZ THIA-MINIs™

BUFFET PROVIDES EXOTIC NUTRIENTS

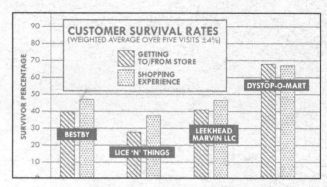

MORE SURVIVORS THAN OTHER STORES

Getting here is $\frac{23}{48}$ the fun! By providently evading the Marauders of Habitable Zone 1 and the mutagenic locust flocks northeast of the Gallup safety district, your approach to the Compound could be without incident.

Upon arrival, take advantage of our freed parking and let the savings begin! Carts and pack animals can be secured to the west-facing parking slope using the provided safety coupling. *Mortice locks are not provided; available for bulk purchase at the Fun Zone.*

SAFE TO VISIT

If an erection lasts more than six hours, dispose of immediately and contact your phrenologist.

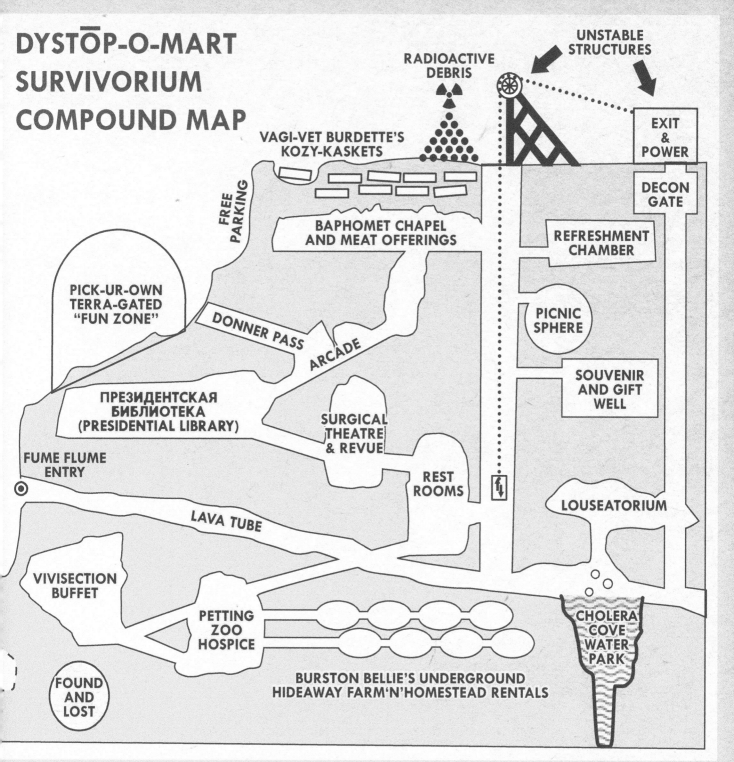

DYSTŌP-O-MART SURVIVORIUM COMPOUND MAP

RADIOACTIVE DEBRIS

UNSTABLE STRUCTURES

VAGI-VET BURDETTE'S KOZY-KASKETS

EXIT & POWER

DECON GATE

FREE PARKING

BAPHOMET CHAPEL AND MEAT OFFERINGS

REFRESHMENT CHAMBER

PICK-UR-OWN TERRA-GATED "FUN ZONE"

DONNER PASS

ARCADE

PICNIC SPHERE

ПРЕЗИДЕНТСКАЯ БИБЛИОТЕКА (PRESIDENTIAL LIBRARY)

SURGICAL THEATRE & REVUE

SOUVENIR AND GIFT WELL

FUME FLUME ENTRY

REST ROOMS

LOUSEATORIUM

LAVA TUBE

VIVISECTION BUFFET

PETTING ZOO HOSPICE

CHOLERA COVE WATER PARK

FOUND AND LOST

BURSTON BELLIE'S UNDERGROUND HIDEAWAY FARM'N'HOMESTEAD RENTALS

HOW TO FIGURE SHIPPING COSTS

The Map Below and Table at Right Will Help You Choose The Best Way To Ship Your Items.

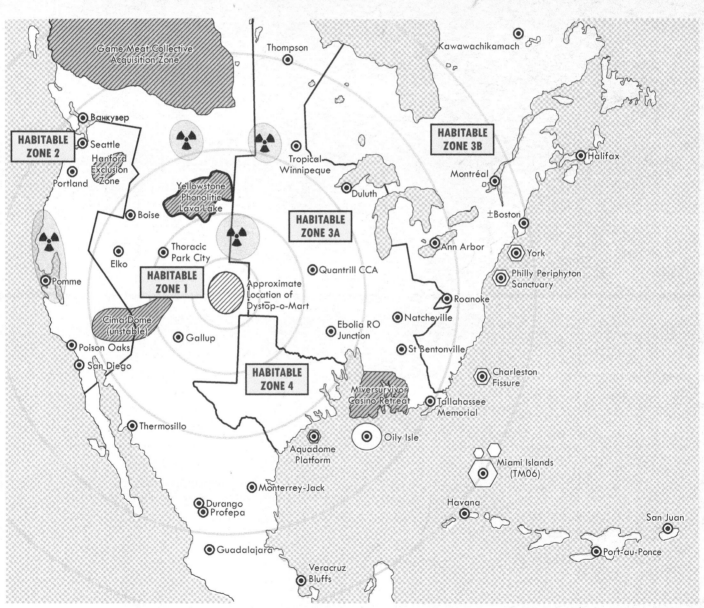

Game Meat Collective
Acquisition Zone

Thompson

Kawawachikamach

Ванкувер

HABITABLE
ZONE 2

Seattle

Hanford
Exclusion
Zone

Portland

Boise

Tropical
Winnipeque

Duluth

HABITABLE
ZONE 3B

Montréal

Halifax

±Boston

Yellowstone
Phonolitie
Lava Lake

HABITABLE
ZONE 3A

Ann Arbor

York

Philly Periphyton
Sanctuary

Elko

Thoracic
Park City

Quantrill CCA

Roanoke

Pomme

HABITABLE
ZONE 1

Approximate
Location of
Dystop-o-Mart

Natcheville

Cima Dome
(unstable)

Gallup

Ebolia RO
Junction

St Bentonville

Charleston
Fissure

Poison Oaks

San Diego

HABITABLE
ZONE 4

Miversurvivor
Casino Retreat

Tallahassee
Memorial

Thermosillo

Aquadome
Platform

Oily Isle

Miami Islands
(TM06)

Monterrey-Jack

Durango
Profepa

Havana

San Juan

Guadalajara

Port-au-Ponce

Veracruz
Bluffs

Items in this catalog are dispatched by geno-sedated pack-bears, smaller caniforms, or dronebots unless otherwise disallowed. Important: please add postage separately for each item ordered and remit full amount. Accepted payment methods include (but are not limited to): pre-end times currencies, platinum, palladium, rhodium, ruthenium, alcohol, shoes, and salt. Due to inconstant economic circumstances, submission of acceptable payment accompanying completed order may not guarantee delivery, and "surrendered" payments to Dystop-o-Mart are not considered retrievable.

Weight (kg)	Zone 1	Zone 2	Zone 3a	Zone 3b	Zone4
1-5	$6.70	$13.33	$18.6_	_21.3_	$31._3
6-10	$12.33	$24.66	_34._	_9	$57._5
11-15	$22.80	$45.62	_6	_8	$__._0
16-20	$42.19	$84.39	$1_.14	$1_.02	$1_.31
21-30	$78.06	$156.12	$2_.57	_79	$3_._8
31-40	NOT AVAILABLE	$_.__	$__._	$_62._1	$6_8
41-5_	NOT AVAILABLE	$354.31	_48._	$854	$1_55.6_
51+	NOT AVAILABLE	_,383.8	$1,581.5_	$2,822.92

MERCHANDISE ACQUISITION FORM
INFORMATION FOR TRANSFER OF CHAIN OF CUSTODY

DATE OF ORDER: Season_____ Trimester_____

CUSTOMER IDENTIFICATION:

MAIN _____

MIDDLE _____

LAST _____

ALIAS _____

MONIKER _____

CLAN (AGNOMEN) _____

NEXT-OF-KIN (max 20 kilometers) _____
_____

IDENTIFIABLE LANDMASS (drainage trench, burial mounds, mixed debris) _____
_____

PARISH/DISTRICT_____

HABITABLE ZONE # ☐ 1 ☐ 2 ☐ 3A ☐ 3B ☐ 4

DRAW A RUDIMENTARY MAP OF YOUR CURRENT RESIDENCE.

☐ CAMP
☐ CAVE
☐ FAVELA
☐ HOVEL
☐ BBU HIDEAWAY
☐ SUPERMAX

YOU ARE HERE

DWELLING TYPE:

☐ Aerostatic Dirigible (Fumed)
☐ Bulk shift containers
☐ Car/Van/Lorry (or Chassis)
☐ Cave (Eolian, Talus) or Grotto
☐ Defense ziggurat (terrestrial or aquatic)
☐ Éolienne Bollée/wind turbine
☐ Fallout Shelter/Garrison
☐ House/Cabin/Lean-to
☐ Injection well, tank, or pit
☐ Lighthouse/Radar Turret

☐ Oil drilling flotation hull
☐ "55 Gallon" Oil Drum (208.197 L)
☐ RV (5th wheel/toy hauler)
☐ Septic Aquaferal System
☐ Silo (Missle/Grain)
☐ Suspension accommodation
☐ Treehouse/Promontory structure
☐ Tubewell drainage pipe
☐ Umiak/Tarai-bune/Gondola
☐ Other (please specify):
_____

CONDITION (Check all that apply):

☐ Abandoned
☐ Adrift
☐ Aloft
☐ En Fuego
☐ Flooded

☐ Functional
☐ Geostationary orbit
☐ Polybrominated Diphenyl Ethered
☐ Irradiated
☐ Other: _____

To promote preventative innoculation of delivery personnel, please indicate any communicable diseases prevalent at your location during the last phaseal term:

☐ Bubonic Craig
☐ ChickenPax
☐ Diphtheria Recall
☐ Ennui-osis
☐ Gamma-Ray-Induced Rage
☐ Haemophilus influenzae Infections
☐ Hepatitis G
☐ Legionellosis

☐ Leptospirosis
☐ Measles™
☐ Meningococcal Infections
☐ Mephitic Miasma Disorder
☐ Non-specific Mutosis
☐ Pertussus
☐ Pneumococcal Pneumonia

☐ Sal Monella Enterica
☐ Schmallpox
☐ Streptococcus
☐ Tawny fever
☐ Tuberculosis
☐ Typhus
☐ Viral hemorrhagic fever
☐ Other:
_____

Acquisition form continues on obverse; failure to complete will invalidate order.

MERCHANDISE ACQUISITION FORM *(CONTINUED)*

PRODUCT INFORMATION

All prices in catalog are stated in Pan-Pacific SinoDollars ($)

MODEL #	PRODUCT NAME	QUANTITY	MINIMUM ACCEPTABLE QUALITY				UNIT PRICE	TOTAL PRICE
			New	Used	Damaged	Parts Only		
_____	_____	_____	☐	☐	☐	☐	_____	_____
_____	_____	_____	☐	☐	☐	☐	_____	_____
_____	_____	_____	☐	☐	☐	☐	_____	_____
_____	_____	_____	☐	☐	☐	☐	_____	_____
_____	_____	_____	☐	☐	☐	☐	_____	_____
_____	_____	_____	☐	☐	☐	☐	_____	_____

LINE 7 (SUBTOTAL): . . . . _____

LINE 8 (SHIPPING COST) (Use chart on page 29 to calculate cost) . . . . _____

LINE 9 (WAR LORD ASSESSMENT) (Multiply Line 7 by .08) . . . . _____

LINE 10 (HABITABLE ZONE SURTAX) (Multiply Line 7 by .075) . . . . _____

LINE 11 (LINE 10 SURTAX) (Multiply Line 10 by 2) . . . . _____

LINE 12 (COMMISSARY TAX) (Multiply Line 7 by .15) . . . . _____

LINE 13 (TOTAL) (Add lines 7 through 12 and write total here) . . . . _____

PAYMENT

TOTAL PAYMENT ENCLOSED:

☐ Monies *(amount)*: _____

or ☐ _____ Kilograms *(specify)*:

☐ Antibiotics
☐ Bite Coin®
☐ Books (Pulped or not)
☐ Candles
☐ Children
☐ Ethanol
☐ Favors
☐ Gold
☐ Honey
☐ Matches
☐ Munitions
☐ Salt
☐ Seeds
☐ Shoe or shoes
☐ Sugar
☐ Tears (fish)

DYSTŌP-O-MART SURVIVORIUM MAXI CATALOG is distributed to

MERCHANTS • WHOLESAILORS • INSURGENCY GUILDS
BRANCH NOMADIANS • OLIGARCHS/NGO ORGANIZATIONS • BLOC PARTIES
INDUSTRIAL RECLAMATION CONCERNS • AD HOCS

ACCESSORIES

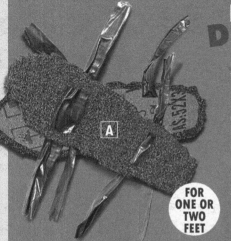

FOR ONE OR TWO FEET

A DR. SHINGLE'S SOLE PATCH

Get the lead out — on the late volcanist Dr. Shingle's ceramic-coated opaque mineral granuloma-filled plates. Strap these heat-resistant asphalt-like planks onto your feet or shoes and soon you'll be bolt'n on the molten — as you attempt to saunter across the local lava patch, and on your way home to the cryptodome. *One size fits all. Do not use if product melts and conforms to heel calcaneus.*

ACC25-09........................ $35.95

B TENSESPEED BY™ LIMBWEAR

The bro-nomenon sweeping the landmass! Robotic limb upgrades are the perfect fit for you, elite athlete! TenseSpeed lightweight prostheses give you the bionic edge-up on hunting, fleeing, and courting. Lightweight antimony ItalioCinese "skeletal" frame comes in colors. Includes polyphenol-tanned leatherette straps for long-lasting, temporary fit. Disarticulator preparation required (see page 46) before using product.

ACC55-207 BIONIC EXTENSION LIMBWEAR CHASSIS............each $3439.00
ACC55-217 MUSETTE/DRAINAGE COMBO (interior/caudal tube not included).... $59.95

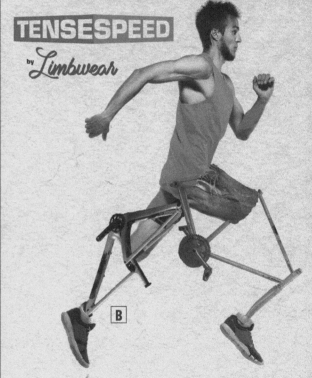

C BIRD WATCH-R

The early bird gets your lice! This tethered-feathered friend peckishly purges those pesky headlice peccadilloes. Three-week lifetime-guaranteed starling is secured to lizard-skinned wrist restraint with untennably-grown hand-assembled Exotic Bur-reed (Sparganium erectum). *Requires feeding for proper operation.*

ACC01-15...$59.95

DYSTŌP-O-MART LABORER SEARCHLIGHT

NAME: Chihp   **POSITION:** Gud Eatz™ Taste Test Survivalist
CURRENT TERM OF EMPLOYMENT: 8 seismic cycles
FAVORITE PART OF JOB: Purging
COMMENTS: "My job is eat product until no more *(chewing noises)*, and make like it don't … *(inaudible)* … allthetime don't smell sometimes because the *(retching sounds)* taste verybad and then don't get selled in the O-Mart store because no good for nuthin." *(collapsing sound)*

GUD 🐐 EATZ

A RACCOON PASTE (PÂTE DE RATON LAVEUR)

Magnifique! This delicious hors d'œuvre combines the quiet simplicity of creamed texture with the biting surprise of the exotic. Essentially de-wormed, and blended with buckrams and other "field green" herbs and spices, our raccoon pâte is the perfect accompaniment on crack'rs, breaded shingles, and scab chips. Whether you're celebrating a successful birth, a harrowing escape, or even just a TGIF rite with horde members, you'll exclaim, "Mierda Sacrée!" after even one bite!

GF91-003..........................$24.95

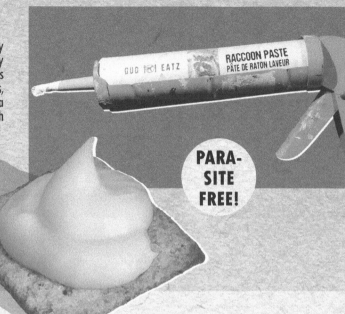

PARA-SITE FREE!

B CHUNK-STYLE SEABIRD MEAT

Delicious chunky chunk-style whitish meat; an acceptable substitute for food! Serve with a glass of warm lactant and a dose of clofazamine for leprosy-lessening, or chop and grind the meat to make delicious "Hoover Hogs," adding warmth to any frosty algid feast.

GF91-005..........................$12.95

GUD 🐐 EATZ

CHUNK-STYLE SEABIRD MEAT

NET WT. / PESO NETO 15.5 OZ (439g)

EDIBLE

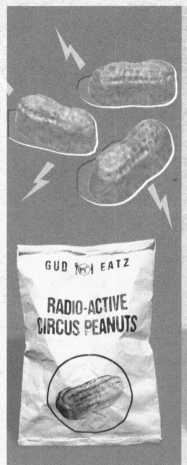

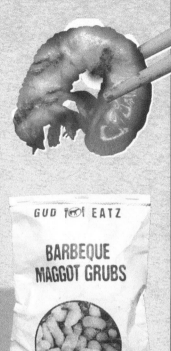

GUD EATZ — RADIO-ACTIVE CIRCUS PEANUTS

GUD EATZ — BARBEQUE MAGGOT GRUBS

GUD EATZ — CHICKEN TARTARE IN SUNDRIED MAYONNAISE

GUD EATZ — NETTLE-FLAVORED PVC CRISPS

C RADIO-ACTIVE CIRCUS PEANUTS
Chewy. 5 to 8 watts per bite.
F058-81 .... $4.95

D BBQ MAGGOT GRUBS
Just like Paw-paw used to eat before he died. Japanese Beetle larvae with authentic cinder flavor.
F058-83 .... $4.95

E CHICKEN TARTARE
Chicken-In-A-Chihp! Presumed sun-dried powdered mayonnaise flavoring leaves a long-lasting, permanent film in your throat.
F058-82 .... $4.95

F NETTLE-FLAVORED PVC CRISPS
Sharp texture with stinging flavor! Eat with caution. Results in unspeakable hallucinations.
F058-84 .... $4.95

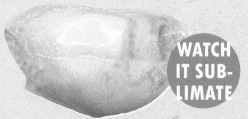

WATCH IT SUBLIMATE

G FROSTBITES™ TRADITIONAL ICED CUBE
500 nanokelvins!! From a square-to-gone in 2 femtoseconds! Educational and exciting! Our own secret recipe solidifies Newtonian fluids from Cholera Cove Artesinal Well, then carefully packages cube for delivery to a location. Even if your offspring have never seen iced water, they won't believe their eye! *Not fit for consumption. For visual entertainment only. Avoid skin contact to prevent life-threatening injury and/or limb loss.*
F412-05 (one 28.4g cube) $13,995.00

FOODSTUFFS

A SNORTABLES LUNCHING POWDERS

It's food for your nose! Dehydrated using cutting-edge phytoradioactive tech, these distinctive prepared meats and legumes can be stored in a variety of meteorological conditions and habitation environments, and remain relatively digestible for any future generations. Before stomach rumbling reveals your hideout to protopredators, open the easy-snap lid, close one nostril, and inhale the tastelike goodness. Your body will appreciate the flavor-full aromas of enriched nutriosimulating supplements reportedly beneficial to functioning organs. Available as multi-pack combo meals. *Will induce morphological and functional changes in the nasal mucosa.*

Combo Meal Combinations:
- KIT A: Dillo Dunkers / Turnip Shards / Kewpie Mayo / Black Tar Licorice
- KIT B: Baloney-Blast'r Corn / Chickweed Bundles / Cassava "Sauce" / Raisin Stemknobs
- KIT C: Purslane-Powdered Lima Beans / Spicy Kale / Garlic or Mustard / Brittled Peenut
- KIT D: Uncured Coyote / Eggcellent Egg-plant / Yarrow Dust / Candied Cane

SNO-401 KIT A $3.95	SNO-403 KIT C $3.95	SNO-406 Extra Portion of Raisin Stemknobs....$1.95
SNO-402 KIT B $3.95	SNO-404 KIT D $3.95	SNO-407 Extra Snort of Yarrow Dust..............$0.95

B OLDE TIMEY TINNED FOODS

Sure they're decorative, but did you know tin drinking cups used to contain edible morsels? Thanks to the finds of Terra-Gated Fun-Zone toddlers on coastal shore reclamation expeditions, you can just taste the past. Singular offerings, sussed by living children!

F750-01 Prestinction "Dolphin Safe"
Rust Tuna $109.95

F750-02 Mixed Artificial Suet $109.95

F750-03 Garden-Flavored Veggie Mash $114.95

F750-05 Maraschino Cherries $119.95

F750-07 Condensed Milk Weed $129.95

F750-12 Private Label Sweet Corn-flavored
Canned Food Product $2.10

F750-14 Yellowed Peaches $324.95

B

C FIBER-RICH FOOD REPLACEMENT THINS

Pre-packaged bundles of cellulose-rich fibers are large in quantity and just might be pleasing to the digestive system. When filleted into small pieces and thoroughly chewed, these resemble consumable food bits, convincing the hypothalamus that you've been fed a nutritious and substantial meal. While preparing the fillets, enjoy mental stimulation and an opportunity to practice reading skills — meditate, then masticate! Sold in 12m² non-waterproof bundles. *Excessive weight charges incurred.*

F550-14............................$795.00

C

Serving Suggestion

FOOD REPLACEMENT EXCREMENT LOAVES* BUYBACK

The more you make, the more you get! As part of our "Excremental Earth" customer rewards program, your nightsoils may brighten the future lives of your kin by returning completed loaves for reprocessing. Simply enclose fresh loaf in a leak-resistant bag, affix approved postage, and within 4-8 seasons your points will be credited to your account. Don't just be a do-gooder; be a "poo-gooder!"

Only solid loaves accepted at this time.

CHOCOLATE RATION HAS BEEN INCREASED

D MAGIC THINKY DRINK

This euphoric beverage is a delicate balance of lymphatic fluids and aromatics luxuriating in a mineral oil base. Consumption accelerates executive functions, leaving the consumer feeling energized, invigorated, and flushed with toxins and mutagenic anomalies. The addition of pomelo extract adds a citrusy splash of sapidity that lingers disingenuously like a poorly-remembered dream. Available in pre-mixed liquid form ready to ingest, or as a powdered concentrate for portability and long-term stowage.

FS165-071 (Liquid: 125ml)..............$49.95
FS165-072 (Powder: 200g)..............$69.95

GOURMET FOODS

Serving Suggestion

JUICY

A BEETLE AU JUS
Our secret, French-bred salpingidae broth starter. Nearly 300 not-yet-extinct species sun-dried and crushed to produce bouillon cakes. Just dissolve in the liquid of your choice to pack a powerful flavor punch! Perfect for slow-cooker Cajun chitins. *Also useful for temporary mortar projects.* Individual: Includes 3-5 adult polyphaga, each 1.5—7 mm in length. Family Bag: May contain up to 20 adult polyphaga.

GOU792-01 .... $29.95
GOU792-04 .... $299.95

B FILLED BURDOCK CIRQUELLES
Intriguingly sweet, muddied flavour; chemically-depurinated so each bite has a distinctively random flavor. We then inject the burrs with a redolent oily filling of transported lingonberry wax, and enrobe the outside with sugared webs. 1 doz per sack.

GOU55-007 .... $23.95

C ±BOSTON PUSTULE SPROUTS
You'll fawn over these delightful sprouts! Genetically-manipulated deer are flavor-blasted with buttery sprout DNA, resulting in a constant supply of Ayurvedic nutrient vegetable nodules. *Promotes tooth decay.*

GOU53-106 (2 kg box) $39.95
GOU53-108 (1 deer).......... $499.95

D KUDZU KAKES
At Kudzuridge Farms, we're harvesting kudzu as fast as our kids can, and turning this wonder plant into eatable treats. But, the fun doesn't stop there——our kudzu keeps growing, even after it's ingested, so one small bite will keep your tummy full for eight days! *To prevent kudzu from harvesting your internal organ mass for growth, consumption of Kudzu Kakes is not recommended.*

GOU53-275 (6 cubes)........ $59.95

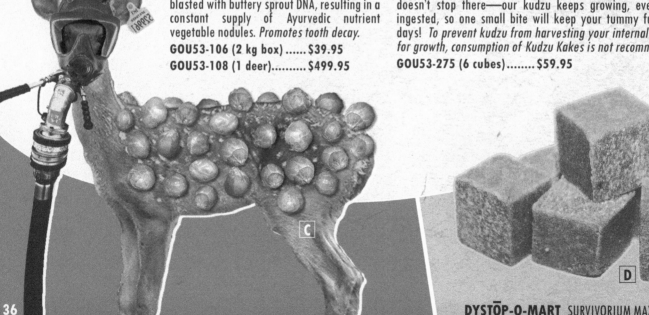

E SESAME SEABORGIUM-106 "BISCUIT"

We put the "RAD" in "bReAD"! Sliced, balled, or toasted, our biscuits will be the mosted delicious bread available in the habitable zone. Seaborgium-106 power eliminates the harmful fungal effects of renegade spores, so it's the yeast with the least! Pathogens, that is! As "safe" for consumption as safe gets.

GOU55-014 .... $15.95

F

IMPORTED FROM TROPICAL SVALBARD

G

H

Serving Suggestion

F NUT BUTTER OYSTER PATÉ

Rocky Mountain Oysters are pureéd and emulsified with firewater and flavorings, then slowly roasted over lava pits to minimize pathogens. To enjoy, spread thinly over toast bark, and ingest for improved mental clarity as well as sympathetic alignment. Limited-edition collectable metal serving container.

GOU53-104 .... $29.95

G SELF-REPLICATING TOMATOE

Flavor that lasts! When exposed to sunlight, our special "tomatoe" uses all-natural cellular mitosis to divide and cultivate. You're assured genetic juiciness without the likely risk from unearthed catsup packets.

GOU55-014 (20 seeds) $18.95

H LANTERNFLY EGG CAVIAR

Imperial taste and complex aroma. Small, smoky grains with a tinge of yellow. Exquisite flavor notes of butter and wharf. Delicious served on our Sesame Seaborgium-106 "biscuits"! Limited quantities available. Favored by new and expectant mothers. 250 gram tin.

GOU55-014 .... $95.00

GOURMET FOODS

A BETEL NUT BAKING MIX

Is your gut bothered by intestinal parasites? Don't call the medicine man/woman; call the muffin man/woman! Use our baking mix for cakes, muffins, spackling, breads, compost pastes, compresses, and gungerbread men/women. Aggressively addictive peppery taste! *Caution: avoidance may prolong lifespan.* 2kg tub.

GOU55-078 .... $14.95

B PUPA-TARTS

Maggot larvae are constrained within fiber-rich cèllulose, then spritzed with decay-heated heirloom energy until bubbling over with mouth-wettening richness. Box of 6 pre-wrapped wafer biscuits.

GOU395-36 .... $22.95

AS SEEN ON

C KUDZURIDGE FARM COOKY ASSORTMENT

The distinctive flavor of kudzu, baked into a delectable treat! We harness the phytogenic power of kudzu, caress with a delicate addition of proprietary flavor enhancers, and finish with thermogenics to bake the might of mitochondria into every tasty bite. One 2kg tin contains three delicious flavors: green, greenish-brown, and "brownish-green."

GOU61-022 .... $24.95

D THERMOPHILIC TARDIGRADE SCAT SNAK

Gelatinated tardigrade flavorings are happily frosted onto a corn-reduction glacé bear scat nougat, with soil-based "spackle" bits for extra crunch, then reconstituted into brickle. Next, a few sieverts of scrumptious energy are added to give each bite an extra "grrrrr!"

GOU10-25 .... $89.95

Push from end for better results

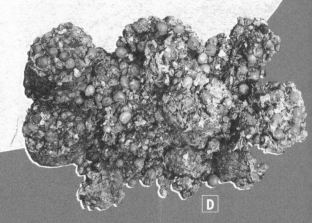

HOUSEWARES

SAFE FOR NOW

E **NON-COMPOSTING FECAL TRAPPER**

Non-composting toilet safely isolates your leavings into one location, reducing fluidic seepage or other osmotic drift. Button-activated lid encapsulates VOCs, HAPs, and other distressing excretae. And, extrae buttons and knobs offer potty-time distractions for little ones while they discharge their toilette.

HW91-003...$49.95

F **GARDEN SHOPPE TERRORIUM**

They may or may not respond to their name. But, they've surpassed their shelf life; you have no accurate indicator of how long they can safely be stored, and what predator risk they pose to you and others who may be living in your Exclusion Zone. The self-feeding, fully-scalable Terrorium PVC cactus defense planter system allows for E-Z maintenance, and keeps the vermin at bay. *Open terroriums are less likely to experience problems with condensation and fungal plant diseases than are closed quarters. PVC cactus may hydrolize during coronal mass ejections.*

GS81-034 UNINFLECTED CACTI
"STARTER CORRAL" (6 ea).................. $495.13

GS81-036 INFECTED GLOCHIDS CACTI
"ENRICHED HOUSING"...................... (market)

GS81-036 SINGLE USE KILLER FROST
"BLANKETS"
(not shown) $289.95

G **BIOACCUMULATOR™ FILTER PRO**

Safer liquids to quench a thirst! Portable, reusable, and reversible. Strains 30kg. Comes in can. Can also be used as spider hatchery. *Do not use to brew bodily fluids or coffee.*

HW91-003 HUMAN HAIRDO................... $49.95
HW91-086 TWO (2 ea) HIGHLY FLAMMABLE
HOT-ROLL CURLING TONGS
IN THREE POPULIST SIZES...$289.95

H **WIND-CURED BRISTLE BRUSH**

Our hands-free-crafted brush with fuzzy carcass wipes away grease and grime, propagated cultures of infectious agents, recombinant/synthetic nucleic acids, phenols, glissandos, and chloroforms, as well as agarose gels containing ethidium bromide. Rostrum beak trills away crusty human/animal bulk blood, tissues, or carcasses, and is handy for awkward post-mortem eyelid closure. Purgation can be music to your ear!

HW91-281... $14.95

39

FOOD PREPARATION

A GLOW-N-GROW RADIOACTIVE SODIUM-22 GROWTH ACCELARUNT

Food supply cutbacks affecting your calorie-consuming posse? Add heat for extra meat! Our unique radioactive lick (now with cyanide sorghum salts!) is mashed into preformulated-wort, where mutagenic properties enable your drove to grow—to mouth-watering heights! Lead acetate adds the sweet rush so popular with kids and kids. Sold in 10 kilo sacks. Feed feeds one livestock unit for three cycles. Glow-n-Grow is gamma-gamma great!

CM90-006 .... $39.95

B FRIDGI-DEERMEAT SMOKING CABINET

Smokes the rot right of the bone — with the only solid-state smoker licensed to bear the Dystōp-o-Mart Seal of Quantity®! Our chain-linked isocyanate and polyol-insulated lead-lined casing encapsulates the heat, scorching-n-torching for weeks! Gravity-fed system uses remaining Earth power to keep combustibles burning upwards. Adjustable shelves and crisper drawers accommodate meats as small as nutria to the largest stuffed dugong.

CM08-71 .... $699.95

C DRIP "COFFEE" BEAN EXTRACTION KIT AND ALL-I.V.

Running for your life or frozen in fear, the best part of waking up alive! Ambulatory or emergent, it's the drop-by-drop way to jumpstart your life. Just be sure to balance the plug-and-play catheter nozzle and put your foot up as gravity does the rest. Single nozzle for beverage; two-way nozzles for intra-venous application. *Beverage "drip tap" and burette with drip chambers not permitted in Ванкувер HZ2.*

CM21-05 .... $129.95

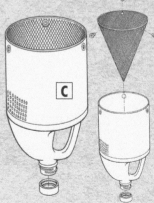

D PERMA-GOATZ™

Keep your Billy fetter-footed for metamilking, pelting, and harvesting. Perma-Goatz is the permanent solv-all for your live-stock stabilizing obligations! Gambrels, noise-cancelling muzzles, and veal vessels sold separately. Our long-lasting organic cementitious compound is moisture-repellent.

CM5181-63 (5 liter plastic sak) $499.95
CM5181-63 (waist-high drum) $19,999.95

E FARMER FIZZ™

These goats take a lickin' and go on sickin'! Farmer Fizz™ takes the best qualities of our Fizz-I-Cyst Effervescent Antibody Restorative (as seen on page 45), and scales vaccine production dramatically upwards in your factory farmward. Your live-stock can now "provide" "health benefits" in "addition" to "edible" meats! Farmer Fizz liquid additive is poured into feed kettles and ingested by live-stock. Watch the concomitant magic of chemistry transform feckless herds into innoculative incubators. Life expectancy grows with every frothy bite!

CM70-61 (not shown) $240.00

F CRANK-OPERATED PIZZA PYRE

This instrument of culinary and funerary opulence represents the apex of eutectic civilization, solving a sundry of food preparation and carcass elimination exigencies. Dynamo-powered oven rewards your perseverance: heat meats, treats, and blackened sweets—just turn the crank, and imagine feasting on baked mouette en croute, toasted moss and seagrass panini, or even palatable carob and acorn mini pies—in only a few precious hours! And, when exuberantly rotated and dry, the furnace diminishes leftover cadavers to ash. Constructed of stucco siding with heat-encapsulating polymeric asbestos interior.

CM14-002 .... $1,399.95

DYSTŌP-O-MART LABORER SEARCHLIGHT

NAME: Samuel **POSITION:** Comfort Threshold Estimator
CURRENT LENGTH OF EMPLOYMENT: 32 seasons
FAVORITE PART OF JOB: Keeping my sup'rvisor living
COMMENTS: "When the SKUs kill a lot of people that's when people stop buying the SKUs and I want the people to buy the SKUs because the more SKUs we sell the more the sup'rs give us free passes so we can cut the lines off at the Fume Flume and that's the best ride at the O-Mart even when I burn every time I ride it but that's like my job so I can raq with that."

G ELECTROSHOQ™ RESISTANT CONDUQTIVE TROUSERS

Amp up your dream of comfort, safety, and convenience while cooking, baking, and disposing family carcasses. Reinforced taintshield and iron mesh lining deflect EMP shoqs away from man parts, while metal inseams conduct the voltage down legs safely towards the ground. Couple with our pimple helmet (see page 54) for flight-to-fork food filleting and flash-frying. Fantastique!

CM09-011 .... $49.95

OFFSPRING MAINTENANCE

4-IN-ONE

F ON-THE-GO-GO BABY CHARIOT

Ride in style! This beautiful conveyance secures one child for transport, and may feature many modern conveniences:

- Sturdy metal frame with welded joints survives drops from heights up to 15 meters
- Two rounded wheels, with heavy-duty Action-Traction™ treads for maneuvering over rocks, bonefields, and lava ash
- Easy, breezy plastic cabin has ventilated holes to keep the child aerated during travel
- Extra-strength repurposed nautical rope fastens the cabin to the frame, and tethers easily to the little tyke's acromioclavicular region.
- Comforting and cushiony tripolar fleece blanket (azure blue, heliotrope, puce, or "sunset" pink) not included.

T2859-26590F $149.95

D MUNITION-RESISTANT BUBBLE O' JOY

A new caliber of daycare…no sniper gets this diaper! Be pro-active, not re-active, with the air-tight impact of an infantry-resistant protective infantile enclosure. Cornerless sphere encourages mobility and exploration, while promising exploration and mobility. Made of transparent moulded acrylic Schneezgard™. *(Will not withstand impact from gatling guns, rotary autocannons, or nematic tephra projectiles. Floats on most non-boiling liquids.)*

P6283-86690 .... $74.95

E TETON TEETHING TEAT / CHEW-TOY STUMPIE

A baby may develop as many as six teeth each, an uncomfortable process for both the child and the ward. This portable device has been known to offer relief. Textured surface encourages dental edging, revealing splinters that gently massage infant's gums. Janka-rated; species may vary. *May contain weevils, rat lungworm, or shrapnel. Suckling logs no longer available.*

P9926-051 TEAT $5.95
P9926-053 STUMP $5.95
P9926-058 SUCKLING $5.95

HEALTHCARE AND BEING

GOOD 4 U
BRAND

A

RADIO-ACTIVE S'PORES

ATOMIC POWER

B

GOOD 4 U
GORGE-US
ANTIEMETIC
ANTI-NAUSEA
SUPPOSITORY
ANA-GEL
5 FL OZ / 147 mL

GOOD 4 U
IRON
SUPPLE-MINTS
MAYBE 200 PIECES

C

B | GORGE-US ANTIEMETIC ANTI-NAUSEA SUPPOSITORY ANA-GEL

Because growing up means throwing up! Between radiation-induced vomiting, infectious gut parasites, and the ever-present toxic miasma, it's hard to keep your meal down. But, food is a scarce commodity, so why waste it?! One generous squirt of our suppository ana-gel is all it takes to keep you from heaving for up to three minutes. Familiar gasoline scent. *Processed in a facility that also produces weapons-grade munitions.*

G4U-1882 .... $29.95

A | RADIO-ACTIVE S'PORES

Say "more" to s'pores—then go with the glow! Enjoy the kaleidoscopic crackle of our pharmelectron collider s'pore nuggets. Add 'em to your favorite liquid source! Use them as topping on mashed pennywort! Place a s'pore between your tooth and gums, and experience the once-in-a-lifetime vibrant flashes for yourself! *Causes permanent auditory hallucinations. Fatal when swallowed.*

G4U-0810 .... $39.95

C | IRON SUPPLE-MINTS

Is your tongue and mouth more than 74.635% red and swollen? *Mbmblmbh...* Are you pale and short of breath? *Uwhoo!* Does your head ache (other than from assaultive concussions)? *Ow!!* How about heart palpitations? *Budum-bum.* Scaly skin and scalp? *Yum!* YOU may be iron deficient—and near death.

The popular diet of fiberboard and cellulotine crackers may not supply the minimum seasonal micronutrients. No need to chew; allow up to 8 seasons for maximum absorption. Hand-picked and carefully sorted. Mint-like, and time-released. *Any ruddy discharges may indicate need for additional serving. May contain nuts.*

G4U-0030 .... $14.95

D FIZZ-I-CYST™ EFFERVESCENT ANTIBODY RESTORATIVE

Sure, for preventative vaccination, we all lick other people's bland-tasting cysts; why not treat loved ones to a fun, flavorful burst? Ingesting Fizz-I-Cyst™ capsules gives your pustules a flavor and taste profile that was, until now, not possible with traditional biological systems. Your dermal excretions will delight with a carbonated, foamy mouth-feel, and exotic flavors will tempt even the most stubborn patient. No more arm-twisting about flavorless cysts to insure the relative survivability of your kin! Now in three flavors: Poultry Marrow, Ginko, & Ackee Fruit.

G4U-35 (Poultry Marrow).. $75.00
G4U-37 (Ginko) $75.00
G4U-38 (Ackee Fruit) $75.00

E GENITAL PASTE

Fungal funk in your mighty junk? Tune up your undercarriage with our patented genital paste! Newly-invented, exclusive formula banishes a myriad of embarrassing inflammations, restoring you as cock-on-the-walk! Bracing ammonia scent. A three-finger dose, applied to private areas every two hours over three lunar cycles offers what can be best described as relief, and a distractive efficacy from bulbous, stinging nodules. May cure: Swamp Rot; Dingleberry Blight; Ring-Around-The-Daddy; Musty Muscle, the dreaded Reef Queef, and more. *Results not guaranteed. Expect skin/hair loss upon application; avoid ingestion and degloving.*
G4U-0026 .... $19.95

F FISSURE FIZZ

The tumescent effervescent! Your skin is all squamous with contaminants and ordure odors. Oh dear! No need for painful enucleation or curretage; one serving of Fissure Fizz will dilate pores to accelerate fatty pus expulsion. Four hours after consumption, use the included dermaplaning rasp to exfoliate. *Avoid open flames for two cycles after use.*
G4U-0790 .... $34.95

DYSTŌP-O-MART LABORER SEARCHLIGHT

NAME: Karyn't **POSITION:** Packing and chipping
CURRENT LENGTH OF EMPLOYMENT: 1.345 cycles
FAVORITE PART OF JOB: Storytime and food
COMMENTS: "The packers are really scary and shouty... and the taping machines has all these sharp teeth that cuts the tape and me but if . . . if, if I don'ts tape the boxes up then all the *high-quality Dystōp-O-Mart products* might falls out."

HEALTHCARE AND BEING

A **HOME SURGERY ACCOUTREMENTS**

Triage centers are nostalgic relics of the past; you are THE first responder for every situation. Be the star of your operating theatre with this all-in-one first-and-last aid kit! 16 items in all.

S0037-M7723.................... $325.95

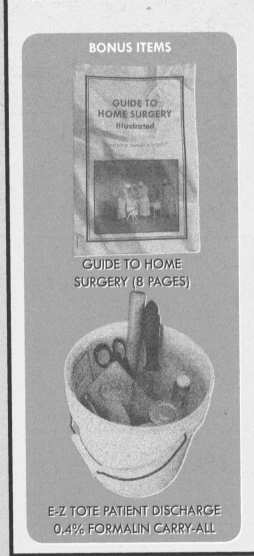

BONUS ITEMS

GUIDE TO HOME SURGERY (8 PAGES)

E-Z TOTE PATIENT DISCHARGE 0.4% FORMALIN CARRY-ALL

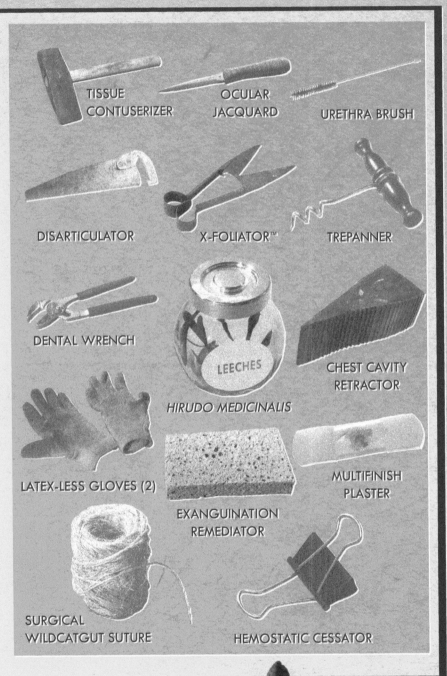

TISSUE CONTUSERIZER

OCULAR JACQUARD

URETHRA BRUSH

DISARTICULATOR

X-FOLIATOR™

TREPANNER

DENTAL WRENCH

HIRUDO MEDICINALIS

LEECHES

CHEST CAVITY RETRACTOR

LATEX-LESS GLOVES (2)

EXANGUINATION REMEDIATOR

MULTIFINISH PLASTER

SURGICAL WILDCATGUT SUTURE

HEMOSTATIC CESSATOR

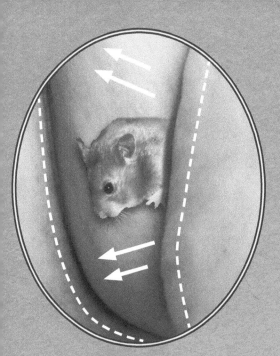

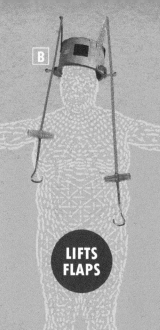

B FLAP-JACK™ RETRACTOR™

Food scarcity and accelerated increases in fight/flight responses lead to extravagant changes in the integumentary system. The decaying panniculus often becomes a hospitable refuge for smaller mammals (especially *rodentia*), reptiles, brown marmorated stenchbugs, and *cimex lectularius* seeking warmth, food, and shelter. With the Flap-Jack™ Retractor™, you can deter future physical infestations — and increase pocketed aeration! — by 136%! Affix retractors to subcutaneous skinfold, then attach suspension cables to the central crown (removing any slack until tensegrity is achieved). Then, enjoy the advent of breezes plus the reduction of peeving predators. *Kit includes crown (head unit); two sharpened, rusticated hooks; and 3m of sturdy decabromodiphenyl ether cables.*

HHS-280 (Complete kit) $129.95
HHS-282 (Replacement hook) $39.95

LIFTS FLAPS

Recom- mended by mid- wives!

C FEMININE HYGIENE PUFFS

Menses making mealtime menacing? Is that lunar lutropin/17α-hydroxyprogesterone scent can enticing your prey to prey on you? Our puffs are the fun-size menstruation cessation sensation crossing the nationstate. Insertable hygiene puffs are snug-fitting and dyed with colors. Puffs are contoured to stay in place — as beautiful on the inside as on the outside. *Pine-scent attracts thirsty mosquitoes.*

HHS-1015 (397 grams bag) $39.95
HHS-1016 (11.34 kilo sack) $699.00

D ANAL LEAKAGE STOP-POMS

Runny runs ruining ration raids? Don't get caught and eaten with your pants down. These lightweight GMO starch-stoppers keep you butt-onned up, eliminating tell-tale trails! Our insertable hygiene puffs are snug-fitting and dyed with colors. Puffs are contoured to stay in place — as manly on the inside as on the outside. *Androstenol-scented to dissuade predation.*

HHS-1017 (387 grams bag) $8.95
HHS-1018 (11.85 kilo sack) $175.00

HEALTHCARE AND BEING

SO MANY USES

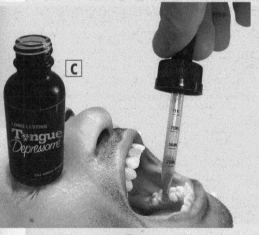

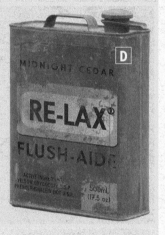

GOOD 4 U

GOOD-4-U BRAND IS BETTER THAN OTHER LEADING BRANDS

Parts are pre-moistened this much before shipping

GOOD-4-U BRAND | OTHER BRANDS

More useful selection of limbs; less filler parts

GOOD-4-U BRAND | OTHER BRANDS

A. ACC-U-PRESS-SURE SWIPHTER
Living in constant fear for one's life can be exhausting! Also at home in your cookhouse, tenderizing and slaughtering foodstuffs in one swift sweep!
HWB-02 (.5m unit) **$249.95**

B. ARMOUR DILL DOUGH
Our family secret takes advantage of the unique properties of these tough little placental mammals. Secret cesium sauce turns the dermal bone scutes into moldable, malleable, self-hardening modeling compound to appease your appetite. Just add water to pre-mixed, artifically-dill-scented crumble, then shape and form; self-irradiating compound provides heat and sets eventually.
HWB-15 (2kg flour sack) **$179.95**

C. LONG-LASTING TONGUE DEPRESSORRÉ
Is your local somniloquist's delirious jabbering robbing you of your precious nightwatch sleep, and putting your whole camp at risk? Is the constant wailing around you a source of annoyance? Apply Tongue Depressorré; just a drop will do ya! It rolls right off (and removes) the tongue, lessening auditory threats and promising a fleeting moment of quietude. *This remedy may be permanent if applied with tongs.*
HWB-72 (15ml tincture vial with dropette) **$79.95**

D. RE-LAX® FLUSH-AIDE
Are lurking predators, felonious bunkmates, and tectonic plates rattling you from your slumber? Rapid rousting from delta sleep patterns might be negatively impacting your z-z-z-zs! Sip into something slumberable — with our prescription-strength oxycodoze soporific soda flush — and flee away to dreamland! Fast-acting and difficult to reverse. Now available in three flavors. *Stains bedding. 500 ml container (not included).*
HWB-51 Salmonberry **$12.95**
HWB-52 Midnight Cedar **$12.95**
HWB-54 Charred Hexapod **$13.95**

E. PIECES 'N' BITS ORGANS AND TIPS ASSORTMENT
Everyone loves surprises! Who couldn't benefit from physical rejuvenation now and then? With our Organ Assortment Mystery Box, limb and organ replacement is twice the fun! Each box is guaranteed to contain at least 45 grams of human organs, limbs, tissue, and other spare bits 'n' pieces. Sealed in corn syrup nutrient flavor, these parts will arrive at your shelter with open arms (included), moist and ready for implantation or ingestion.
HHS-991 .... **$379.95**

DYSTŌP-O-MART SURVIVORIUM MAXI CATALOG

COSMETICS

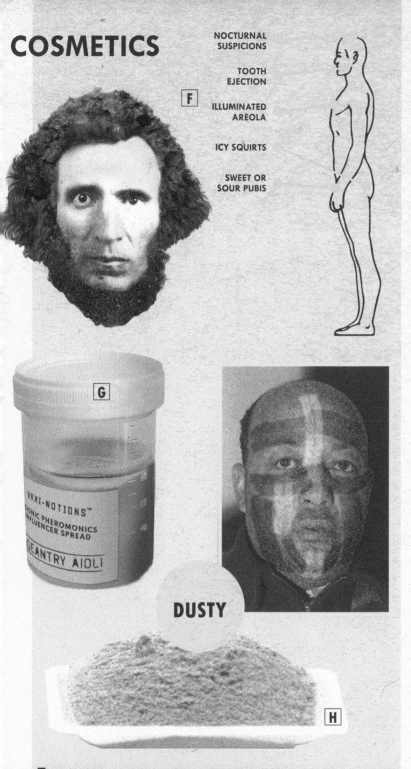

NOCTURNAL
SUSPICIONS

TOOTH
EJECTION

F

ILLUMINATED
AREOLA

ICY SQUIRTS

SWEET OR
SOUR PUBIS

DUSTY

F HAIR REPLACEMENT NESTING FLUFF

Ambient gamma radiation is an omnipresent cause of hair loss and alopecia areata. Our multi-hued fluff hides dangerous reflective baldness! Soft, pliable reclaimed microfibers propose a hardier appearance, and simultaneously provides a suitable nesting burrow for small animals, luring them for companionship and/or easy snacking. Multi-hued fluff affixes to exposed dermis with saliva, sap, or pitch. *Hyper-allergenic.*

HW91-13 (Gray, 200g bag) $29.95
HW91-15 (Black, 200g bag) $39.95
HW91-16 (Potpourri, shown on left, 200g bag)...... $34.95

Not Pictured: **MERKINBOT ACCESSORY FOR GENITAL SUSPENSOR & FACE MASK (See page 19)**
Attaches fluff neatly to sticky-stripes for luxury camo concealment. Kit includes one jar of wasp honey, applicator rag, instructive illustration, and free warning label.

HW91-25 .... $69.95

G VAXI-NOTIONS™ PSIONIC PHEROMONICS INFLUENCER SPREAD

Our pheromonal behavioral spreads and "sandwich" toppings induce recipients into a myriad of unexpected actions and desires. After placing just one spoonful into the mouth region, micro-biome activators take immediate hold of limbic structures, enhancing brain chemistry for intentional results!

HW91-93 (Induces fear of mixed plaids) $19.95
HW91-95 (Desire to perform menial labor) $49.95

For stronger, faster-acting results, try the deluxe More-Onic! Simulated "eggy" mayonnaise flavor is fatty and palatable.

HW91-57 (Tumultuous serenading/pageantry) $69.95
HW91-51 (Projectile propellant precision)....... $89.95
HW91-54 (Increased alphabetization skill).... $129.95

H ENERGIZED SKELEDUST AMALGAM

Irradiated bonemeal is resurrected as a handy scrubbing compound. Acute solar exposure from airbursts induces accelerated stratification, facilitating bone devolution into our pristine powdered meal. Mix with arborvitae oil. Positively charged alpha (α) particles attract viruses and pathogens in a jiffy. Apply powder in a circular motion to problematic areas, using a handheld carcass; expect miraculous results within 4 to 6 cycles of scrubbing. *Arborvitae oil not available in most Habitable Zones.*

HW91-285 1 kilogram sack $18.95
HW91-286 Carcass (mixed, unspecified)............ $0.89

WORLD ~OF~ BOOKS

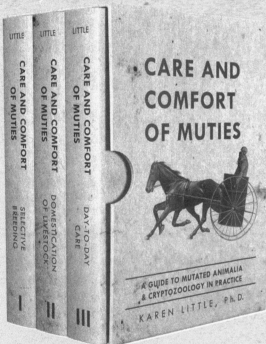

LITTLE — CARE AND COMFORT OF MUTIES — SELECTIVE BREEDING — I

LITTLE — CARE AND COMFORT OF MUTIES — DOMESTICATION OF LIVESTOCK — II

LITTLE — CARE AND COMFORT OF MUTIES — DAY-TO-DAY CARE — III

CARE AND COMFORT OF MUTIES

A GUIDE TO MUTATED ANIMALIA & CRYPTOZOOLOGY IN PRACTICE

KAREN LITTLE, Ph.D.

A | CARE AND COMFORT OF MUTIES: A GUIDE TO MUTATED ANIMALIA & CRYPTOZOOLOGY IN PRACTICE

With a bevy of chemical agents, radiation exposure, and rogue genetic manipulation, evolutionary biology has accelerated at a thrilling pace. It seems new species emerge every day, with innovative repercussions. Regionally-renowned biohealer Dr. Karen Little collects her own sizable relationships with muties into this boxed-set reference work, explaining how she co-exists with nature's latest breakthroughs. New addendum includes: whip and flog communication; inter-species sexual congress; "friend or food?"; harvesting extraneous appendages; and much, much more.
BUK81-021 .... $1,899.95

Words That Rhyme with **PPY**

as told to Rev. Burston Bellie

a Cassowary reader

B | WORDS THAT RHYME WITH PPY

AS TOLD TO REV. BURSTON BELLIE
The book that's taken the continent by chemstorm! The biggesppy fadppy nippy in an Anthropoceneppy!
BUK51-09 .... $29.95

CRAFTING *with* **POISONS**

Recipes for Disaster

by ANNIE, WHO LIVES IN THE CAVE (NOT THE ONE BY THE OLD STEEL MILL)

C | CRAFTING WITH POISONS: RECIPES FOR DISASTER

It's never to early to master chemistry, especially when species survival is at stake! Your offspring will cotton how to stealthily disarm, debilitate, and destroy their enemies using simple, all-natural ingredients provided with love by Mother Nature. Includes all-new pages on becquerel diets and mystical considerations.
BUK81-042 .... $11.95

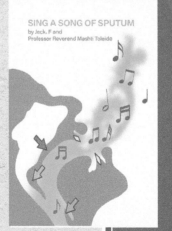

SING A SONG OF SPUTUM
by Jeck. F and
Professor Reverend Mashti Toleido

D | SING A SONG OF SPUTUM

BY JECK. F AND PROFESSOR REVEREND MASHTI TOLEIDØ
Traditional sacrificial psalmighty sing-along fun for your mulching band or campfire diaspurim. Singout lewd ease!
BUK81-024 .... $29.95

Books for kids

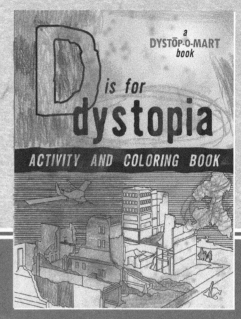

E **PUT ME IN YOUR MOUTH:
A CHILDREN'S GUIDE
TO EDIBLE VERMIN**

When dinnertime is finder's keepers, your kin had better know the difference between food and foe! Teach them to eat hearty with this instructive book by Billy, the Zone-renowned chef whose riverside café has fed customers for lustrums. Bonus pages on flavored parasites and defensoinstructive techniques. *Illustrated.*
BUK81-041 .... $11.95

F **MY FIRST SLAUGHTER:
SURVIVING ON YOUR OWN,
LEVEL ONE: AGES 4—8**

Parents eaten by wolves? There's no need for you to go hungry, little Charitie! The keys to survival are right at your fingertips! Lessons on shelter, food prep, and mass graves are explained in a playfully kid-friendly, step-by-step manner. *Includes butcher charts for 14 species.*
BUK81-044 .... $12.95

G **D IS FOR DYSTOPIA:
ACTIVITY AND COLORING BOOK**

Learn the alphabet, the Dystōp-o-Mart way! Each page contains an image for coloring, along with other words. And, activity pages stimulate the mind without stressful cerebral impact. The perfect gift for toddlers and doomsayers.
BUK51-917 .... $11.95

H **RADIONUCLIDES
FOR FUN & PROFIT**

BY THOR E.M. "THEDDY" THORIUM
Sooner or later, the odor will confirm that she's dead and gone. But her worth isn't! This enriching step-through guide will blind you with the secret of weaponizing and profiting from every sizzling sievert of her remains. Swearing your love comes fuel cycle!
BUK54-03 .... $249.95

I **FINGER FOOD
Hypothermeal Recipes**

EDITORS: BILLY T.C.G.B.T.R. ET AL.
Our favorite fleshipés from around the Zones — transcribed from the pockets of Mrs. Barrelsville Edwinston's deceased sous-chefs — make for a refreshingly chewy nosh. Perfect for dining on the run and absolute-zero ceremonial assemblies. Get your meat hook on a copy asap. *"Two thumbs, sunny-side up!"*—VV Burdette
BUK24-2 (Paperbound) $69.95

TOYS

A **CRÈCHE-COURSE INCUBATING OVEN EXPERIENCE**

Playtime, transformed! Your child's innate affinity for nature and the odds of survival is elevated into a life-learning experience with this three-in-one product. Front-facing access lid allows easy entry for the tyke to sit, ponder, and hide, with some sense of comfort in the artisinally-designed protective safe space. Later, filling the enclosure with burning embers turns the playroom into a combination baking oven and outer cooking/searing surface. Third, the blistering oven becomes an incubator for bat eggs, while the exterior may be an attractive final nesting place for potentially edible hot snakes and other reptiles. *Not designed in sterling silver with gold vermeil accents.*

CT-920.............................. $129.95

GREAT FOR BATS

B **STAIN SETTER**

For use with Incubating Oven Experience. Children love using it for hours! Heated metal, when applied to insect paste, helps set blood stains for a more personalized look, sure to intimidate aggressors. Reportedly used as a peagle press or squid immobilizer.

CT-922...................... $19.95

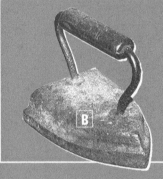

C **SHADY-DAY EXPRESSION COLORING NODULES**

The typhoon has not let up for six cycles; most vegetation and farmstock have washed away. And, worse, your kids have an insufferable case of cabin fever! Before you do something you just might regret, reach for an expression nodule! Marrow and locally-harvested COPCs are integrated into a paste, then conglomerated with cinnabar, arsenic, and Prussian Colbalt-60 Blue for varied pigmentation. Set of 8 blocks. Color assortment and pigmentation-level not guaranteed. *Exposure of nodules to humidity may result in discoloration and/or catalytic fulmination.*

CT-030.............................. $8.95

D **BYGONE BUREAUCRACY COLORING PAPIER**

Delightful pre-printed sheets of rare vintage papier offer a surface for drawing and documentation. Impenetrable historical dictates such as "Form B2830 — Chapter 13 Debtor's Certifications Regarding Domestic Support Obligations and Section 522(q)," "Form B104 — For Individual Chapter 11 Cases: The List of Creditors Who Have the 20 Largest Unsecured Claims Against You Who Are Not Insiders," and "ADB: Accelerated Death Benefit" are sure to stimulate neocortex functioning. Junior litigants will enjoy deliberating and deciphering the meaning of these enigmatic phrases. Complex patterns and letterforms amuse children and the enfeebled for minutes at a time! *Should not be used as incontinence briefs.*

CT-153 (10 sheets) $3.95

E BOX OF SPIDERS

Young pioneers convene with nature and nutrition with this wonderful, self-contained learning lab! Spiders are raised in the Surgical Theatre & Revue, where they live and grow in abundance beneath mildew-rich, soured mattresses. Then, we curate our selection of the most agile of the clutter, and package them in an heirloom-quality "reliquary", ready to be discovered or loved by your kin. Also makes a perfect gift for conquest anniversaries, Rumva celebrations, or unforseen births. Many of the spiders will arrive alive. *Caution should be exercised in handling as poisonous residues may liquify. Packaged by weight, not volume; settling will occur during transit.*

CT-038...**$79.95**
CT-039 EXTRA LIVE SPIDERS (1 dozen) **$8.95**
CT-041 EXTRA DEAD SPIDERS (4 dozen).......... **$3.95**

F BALANCE BOXES

Counteract feebility with strength training! Child-sized boxes, when filled with debris, provide stimulating exercise — and productive merrymaking. When used 16-21 hours per day during daylight harvest season, fit-bodied children can learn essential skills, develop hand-eye coordination, and contribute to the collective good of the populace. Kit includes two wooden and/or plastic and/or mammalskin boxes/crates/bins/sacks, with comfortable and/or uncomfortable leatherine and/or nylon and/or chainlink straps. *Box contents and child included with purchase.*

CT-210...............................**$39.95**

G LEARNING GEL

What can it be? Can it mature into a sour gas? Will it devolve into a luminescent foam? Should it combust when exposed to light? Can I eat it? Will I feed it to others? Learning has never been more exciting. *Volatile compounds may exhibit negative formative enthalpies.*

CT-703 (1 litre) **$42.95**

H ANGRY ANGRY HIPPO BEETLES

Rhinosimus is ready for lunch! This exciting game for one "player" turns hunting for food into an excitably competitive and repetitive challenge! Overhand capturing motion stimulates flexor tendons. Also works with chapulines; olé! Kit includes capture pod and organically-grown cudgel switch. *Some assembly required; adhesive not included.*

CT-441...............................**$19.95**

SPORTING GOODS

A CROQUET TENDER-GAME GAME

Your kin will howl as Auntie swings at the fowl! You'll feast on the splendor of a meal that's so tender. Why suffer decayed when there's freshly pureéd! Good for restoring motor skills and potentially procuring easily-digestible protein sources. *Not advised for prey that exhibits lyssavirus mutantcies, is easily provoked, or is alive.*

SPG-5161.. $89.95

FOR EGGS

B EGGQQUISITION SUSPENSION SYSTEM

Combines the death-applying thrill of abseiling with the time-honored desire to feed! Antagonized aircraft cable and balancing hoist uses intermittent gravity to help suspend you above agitated prey, while your family lowers you to quickly grab eggs and remains. Attempting to escape the incensed gator-mom below is a super family-bonding upper-body exercise!

SPG-095 (4 meter length) $79.95

Cutting Board Included

C TRADITIONAL PICKELHAUBE BIRDING HELMET

Getting bombarded by a flailing flock of asphyxiating birds is never a walk in the park. Why not turn this everyday occurrence into sport and, perhaps, lunch! Don our ProTkt-branded version of the beloved pimple hood pickelhaube helmet; position yourself under the fallway, and presto! Birds lance themselves onto the medal spit, and out of the grabby hands of other birders. Can also be used as an aggressive birder deterrent. Track your catch on the included reversible Cutting Board Pro (sedimentary carbonate drawing utensil/tourné knife not included). *Carcasses must be laboriously examined for toxic carbonyl and anhydrous stains, which may affect taste. ACCESSORY MUST NOT BE WORN DURING ATMOSPHERIC ELECTRICAL DISCHARGE AS DISCOLORATION MAY OCCUR. Guaranteed sawing spark-erosion.*

SPG-61 (Helmet and Cutting Board Pro kit).. $139.95

D HYPER-CØOLED SLITHERSKËES®
Why walk, when you can glide? The termination of genetic reptilian advancements means a surplus of reliably intelligent squamates. Just secure to your footwear or feet, suspend a lure (sold separately), and hold tight for the fastest, slitheriest mode of glacial travel. Available in budget-conscious venomous version, or de-fänged GE edition (for less-worrisome, upscaled recreation). *Not recommended for traversing lava fields or heterogeneous nucleatory glacial growths.*

SPG-67 (Venomous) $139.95
SPG-68 (De-fänged GE) $219.95

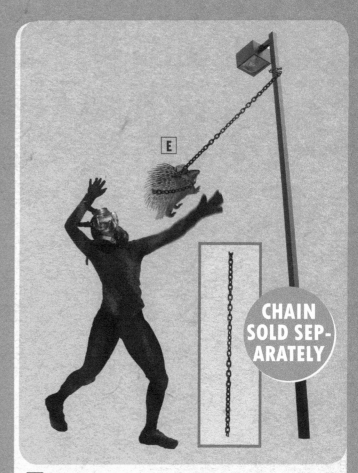

CHAIN SOLD SEP- ARATELY

E PORCU-BALL
Mass flash-frost kill-off? What a prickly mess! Finally, a recreational use for "freeze-dried" porcupines! This pointedly pleasant recreational pasttime will provide your progeny — from tweens-to-toddlers — with fear-filled feats for family fun.

SPG-381 (preserved porcupine carcass) $129.95
SPG-381 (1m length of chain) $8.95

DISTRACTIVES

A FLIPPYBOOK VISUAL/ DEXTERIAL STIMULATOR

The world in motion, at your fingernubs! Relieve the memories of the past, experience the promise of yesterday's tomorrow, or peek under the kimono of the furthest-recorded Zones. Digitally-activated image sequences simulate cerebral synaptic functions, while storylines assuage the senses.

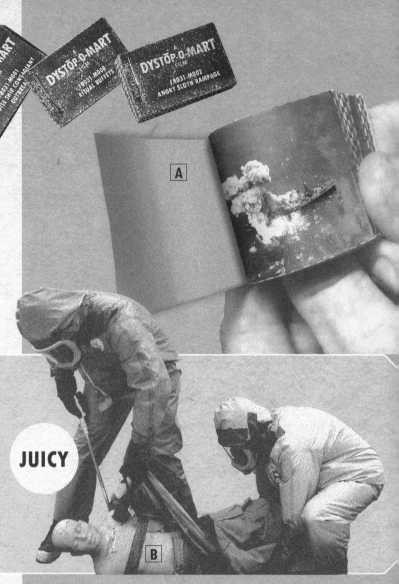

FB031-1 CRUISE SHIP CONTAGIANT OUTBREAK....	$14.95
FB031-2 ANGRY SLOTH RAMPAGE	$14.95
FB031-3 LOVE FOR THE BATTLEFIELD	$14.95
FB031-5 UNFORTUNATE JUNGLE TOMB	$14.95
FB037-6 ROMANCING THE CLAMS......................	$14.95
FB037-8 RITUAL BUFFETS..................................	$14.95
FB038-2 MILITARY SURPLUS SHIP HIJACK	$14.95
FB038-4 KANGAROO COURTING (*adult content*)...	$14.95

B LASSY-CUM-HOME PERSONAL EVENT APPARATUS

Everybody needs a friend! Are decomissioned social humanoid servants washing up and startling the little ones at the Dystōp-o-Mart Terra-Gated FunZone? Our staff quickly harvests these former citizens from the greedy hands of frightened children, and modifies them to be more of a "personal assistant". De-wired for maximum, highly-pliable resin silkiness, personal appetites are satisfied without pretense or aggravating negotiation. Size/gender based on availability and not guaranteed. *Refurbished stock. Due to possible use as an aquatic animal habitat, use caution when entering.*
DIS-760 ....$399.95

JUICY

C BIZZY-BEES™ CARRY-ALL TATTOO PARLORAMA

You betcha beeswax you'll have fun with these longer-lasting, genetically-enhanced Open Pipe Mud Daubers! Obtain a printed image of your choosing (sold separately), apply the image to the desired skin/bone area, attach the OPMDs. If you somehow remain motionless for 3-4 hours, you'll have the avimprint pierced into your dermis! Jar good for repeated individual applications (based on OPMD lifecycle). Tattoo duration may vary. *Sharing jar with others is discouraged. Daubers are not edible. Not safe for scarification or cicatrisation.*
DIS-85 .... $45.95

APPLY IMAGE

ATTACH BEES

REGRET CHOICE

PRESENT CORNER

'TIS THE SEASON

D GIFT BAG

Our festive curated collection of post-historic hand-harvested containment wrappings. Choose from scented or unscented. Non-sealing tops allow for humidity equalization and easy-in, easy-out accessibility. Can be used as one-of-a-kind beverage vessels or protective hand covering for neutron showers. *Sturdy construction of biaxially oriented polypropylene (BOPP), low-density polyethylene (LDPE), and thermoplastic resin. Assorted sizes.*

SHO-081 .... $45.90

E MIXED MEDIATORS

Don't lose your head at the next ritual ceremony! Offers holiday or everyday protection.

SHO-005 "I, AMULET"
(1, assorted)

..........$23,459.95

SAVE (1.345% with promo code 'SURVIV@L'

JUST MIGHT WORK

NEUTRON TURNS ME ON!

G VAN-DER-WAALS™ BRAND GRAVITY TESTER PROBES

The catastrophic success of 126 networks means disruptive sensations and vertiginous tensor fields affecting gravitational stability! Our testing probes neither confirm nor deny the presence of gravitational attraction, which otherwise would help avoid public plummets, fatal falls, and incapacitating incontinence. Ovum-shaped and relatively easy to transport and deploy, Van-der-Waals™ probes are precisely calibrated to a standard gravity of 9.80665 m/s², for consistent results and outstanding experiential repeatability. Shipped in hand-cured histoplasmotic baskets. Single-use only.

GR2-005 PROBES (One dozen)......... $59.95

GR2-006 PROBE (One, locally-poached) $8.95

GR2-008 PROBE REGENRATOR
(*Gallus gallus domesticus* model,
not pictured) $389.95

GRAVITY CORNER

You'll flip out over our goods!

HANG IN THERE, MAYBE

F TUF-GUY PRY-LYE ADHESIVE HAND KREME

Clinging to surfaces to avoid predators doesn't need to be such a botheration. Pry-lye Kreme deeply dilates skin pores to extend the flaws of physics — and vice-visceral. Upon contact with exposed skin, Pry-lye triggers an radical dermal contraindication, transforming connective tissue into a hyper-responsive agglutinant. Scale walls, dangle from girders, and grasp branches until danger wanes. *Surface bond becomes permanent with 30 seconds; after bonding, reach for our bone DISARTICULATOR (see page 46).*

GR4-38 (.3L bag of lotion).....$65.00

Get 'em while-u-last!

SINUS IRRIGATION ASPIRATOR (SIA)

OvertlyAggressive™ mask uses highly-effective suction to remove paranasal parasites in sputum secretions. Ask your nucleolaryngeal healer if SIA treatment is right for you. *Not to be applied to multiple orifices simultaneously. May experience Naegleria fowleri incubation after use. Deadly when used on children.*

CL-455 Adult............................. ~~$49.95~~ $19.95

CL-456 Children/Livestock .... ~~$49.95~~ $19.95

DEFENSE DECOY END TIMES TABLE

One glimpse at this durable rack of IEDs, and marauders will pillage elsewhere to steal a meal. Keep away from combustible objets d'art and unconscionable geothermal heat.

CL-172..... ~~$240.00~~ $19.99

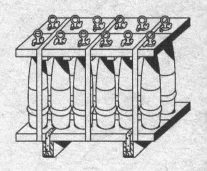

CUP-A-TOE REGENERATION PORRIDGE BY BEYOND FEET™

What better way to walk away from unpleasant amputation than to regenerate! With today's modern podiaradiative exposure, customers are reporting cases of unstoppable phalangengeric regeneration. "Toe the line" with home-grown nutrition.

CL-387......... ~~$400.00~~ $399.95

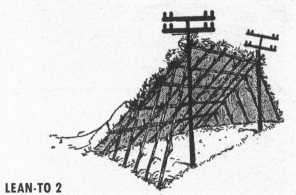

LEAN-TO 2

Innovative pop-up telecommunication totemic systems suitable for product vendors, consummation ritualling, and limited shelteration. *Only available in Hazard Zones 060-085.*

CL-208............. ~~$89.95~~ $29.95

BURR-EATO

Sandspurs may be poisonous, but they may be able to help nutritional needs in a pinch. Wrapped in recycled locally-sourced paper pulp or similar. *¡Peligroso!*

CL-015............................. ~~$12.95~~ $1.95

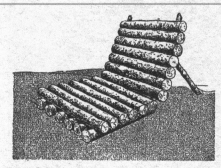

LOUNGE LIZARDS

The recent reptile nurseries fad led to a return to simple incubationary solutions. Moisten "log" to allow reptiles to slink into hand-made multi-material "log" surfaces and crawlspaces. **Cobra Advisories have "log"ged product recalls... get yours before you can't!** Reptile eggs and molting pelage sold separately.

CL-38 .... ~~$49.95~~ $59.95

SALAD SALLET
The penultimate in personal food security. May be conductive to surviving species of microradicchio, macropea shoots, microdurian, lingering arugula, and wheatgas. Helmet must be removed nightly to avoid root scalpogermination via hair follicles.

CL-110...............~~$39.95~~ $9.95

HORNET-POWERED PORTA-SPRINKLER
This spin-and-spray prototype uses excited Mandarinia Smith hornets (not included) to inject liquid into cement dispenser globe.

CL-54 (Sprinkler)...............~~$79.95~~ $19.99
CL-55 (Hornets).................~~$24.95~~ $3.99

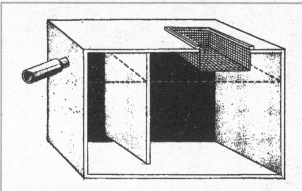

LICEATORIUM
Fill the metal grid tray with hair clippings and scabs. Lice come to feed, then cascade into the greased chamber, which will fill in days! Then, introduce a flame to nozzle. Ashen lice remains can be used to dust oily patches of skin or flooring.

CL-290.............................~~$170.00~~ $99.95

CATHETER SUIT
For safer dispensment of radio-compromised body fluids. *For ages 1 and up.*

CL-224................~~$14.95~~ $6.99

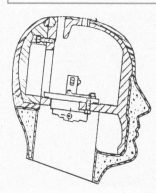

SILHOUETTE SPYHOLE
Who's that? Not you! They'll never know! Survey them while cloaked behind this hand-held peek-a-profile *pop-up. Adds* virtual privacy sensation during use. Not bullet, stinger or chemical weapon-proof.

CL-071................. ~~$8.95~~ $2.95

INFLATABLE SURROGATE WIFE
Next time you need to exert your emotional intelligence, shop Dystōp-o-Mart! An injured female can create numerous risky logistical problems; this mealworm-and-metal blow-up punching torso may just be the convenient equivalent for showcasing your alpha dominance.

CL-281.....................~~$129.95~~ $19.95

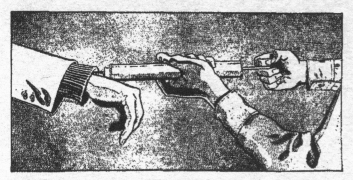

SUPER GOO TENDON STRENGTHENING GLUE
Suffering from radioactive forearm fricassée? Add glue to sleeves or other to create a permanent bond that may increase arm strength and mimic skeletal "structure." Cut clothing off to remove. *Applying on neck areas of garment discouraged.*
CL-441 (250g tube)........... ~~$125.00~~ $3.95

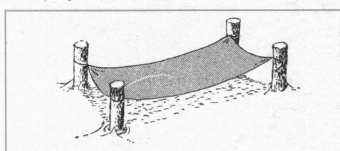

INFANT/AMBULATORY BASSINET
Durable Woven galvanized concertina wire. Stakes not included. *Discontinued.*
CL-175 (Used and Refurbished)   ~~$24.95~~ $9.99

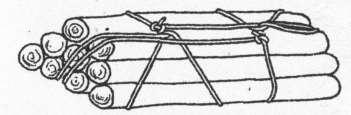

BATTERING RAM WITH SHOULDER STRAP
Wire-bound plumbing tubes pack a wallop.
CL-908.............................. ~~$39.95~~ $24.95

ENDOFF PUBLISHING AND COLLECTION EDITIONS Fifth Quarter

Copyright © DYSTOP-O-MART Communications By Staff

All rights resurfaced under relational government jurisdictions of CitiChase Limited Habitational Treaty and Conflict Prospectivus. New Wichita, HabiZone 3-4.5.

Originally published as legal verification for GED.D and PTSD curriculum and certification. Not liable for discrepancies in alphanumeric nomenclature and divergences from regional colloquial linguistics.

Published in or near New Northern Hemisphere by Hexagram Hut, a division of Congeneric Consumer ConsulTents Corp.

"Dystōp-o-Mart", "Barrelsville Village", "PICK-UR-OWN", "Personal Transportation Pod", "PROTKT", "HOOFERS Holding Limited, "Scaly Plasitpedic", "GUD EATZ", "GOOD-4-U", "CHOLERA COVE", "VAGI-VET BURDETTE'S, KOZY-KASKETS", "BURSTON BELLIE's UNDERGROUND HIDEAWAY FARM -N- HOMESTEAD", "FUME FLUME™", "FECAL DRIFT", "FOOD", and the number 4 are registered tirademarks of DYSTOP-O-MART Communications Corp..

Grateful acknowledgment is due to the following for permission for product promotion: Long Last Funerary Opportunities Association, Farm Freshened Fauxfood, AAA Safe Prenatal Constructions.

The Dr. & Mrs. Barrelsville Edwinston THANKS-Ā-LIMB™ Organ Donors
Mr. Tim Sacco • Chris "Primate Savior" A. • Jean Enrica & Burnsy
Occasionally Honorable John C. Wilson • Robert Heuer • Gurin & Kallins Co.
Lord Cohen — King of the Zoetropes • The Ranis Family Proper
Heather Woodfield • P.M. • C.J.P. • J.J.

ISBN 979-8-9865794-0-5

a
DYSTŌP-O-MART
book
dystopomart.com

SURVEILLANCELOT BRANDSCAN® TRADE MARK

Endure the Dystōp-o-Mart Survivorium at **dystopomart.com**
Printed in the United States of America

10 9 8 7 6 5 4 3 2 1

Lightning Source UK Ltd.
Milton Keynes UK
UKHW020623091222
413588UK00009B/128